1000

By
Salem Kirban

Library of Congress Catalog Card No. 72–97136

ISBN 0–89957–901–9

FUTURE EVENTS PUBLICATIONS

Published by Future Events Publications, an imprint of
AMG Publishers, P. O. Box 22000, Chattanooga, TN 37422.

Printed in the United States of America
02 01 00 99 98 97 –D– 10 9 8 7 6 5

CAST OF CHARACTERS

RESURRECTED BELIEVERS

Helen Omega: Wife of George Omega. Helen, with her two children, were caught up in the Rapture prior to the Tribulation Period.

Sue & Tommy Omega: Children of George and Helen Omega.

Tom Malone: Was Presidential Secretary to Brother Bartholomew in the Tribulation Period. Because of his Christian testimony, however, Brother Bartholomew snuffed out his life with a death ray from a laser gun.

Bill Sanders: Husband of Faye Sanders. Bill was the first person to die by guillotine in the Tribulation Period because of his Christian testimony.

LIVING BELIEVERS who went through the Tribulation Period

George Omega: Husband of Helen Omega. TV news commentator.

Faye Sanders: Wife of Bill Sanders and daughter of George & Helen Omega. Faye, experienced the trials of the Tribulation Period along with her father, George Omega.

Terry Malone: Wife of Tom Malone. She went through deep trials in the Tribulation Period.

Sylvia Epstein: Wife of Abel Epstein.

OTHER CHARACTERS

Brother Bartholomew: Antichrist. Powerful world leader in the Tribulation Period.

Dr. Curter: Scientist. He, amid the Tribulation Period, had preserved Brother Bartholomew's body in a deep freeze cyro-capsule and eventually rejuvenated him.

Abel Epstein: Husband of Sylvia Epstein. Inventor of the Ruby Laser.

Walter Brinks: Executive in World Television Network.

Harry Sutherland: Vice-President of World Television Network.

Carole Sutherland: Wife of Harry Sutherland.

Phil Sutherland: Nephew of Harry Sutherland.

Esther Sanders: Daughter of Bill and Faye Sanders.

Bart Malone: Son of Tom and Terry Malone.

CONTENTS

ACKNOWLEDGMENTS

To **Dr. Gary G. Cohen,** Professor of Greek and New Testament at Biblical School of Theology, Hatfield, Pennsylvania, who carefully checked the final manuscript and supplied many helpful suggestions which have been incorporated in this book.

To **Frank Nofer,** artist, who skillfully designed the front cover.

To **Dick Miller,** artist, who captured many of the events in this book in illustration form.

To **Robert Krauss,** who coordinated all the art work and designed the charts.

To **Doreen Frick,** who devoted many hours to proofreading the text.

To **Batsch Company,** for excellent craftsmanship in setting the type.

To **Walter W. Slotilock,** Chapel Hill Litho, for making many of the negatives necessary for printing.

To **Dickinson Brothers, Inc.,** for printing with all possible speed and quality.

To **Diane Kirban,** H. Armstrong Roberts and many other photographers who pooled their resources so that we may have photos that convey the message of this book.

All Scriptures verses used, unless otherwise identified, are from the King James Version of the Bible.

The New American Standard Bible (ASV) By Permission of The Lockman Foundation.

The Amplified New Testament By Permission of The Lockman Foundation.

The Amplified Old Testament, Part 1, Copyright © 1962 by Zondervan Publishing House. Used by Permission.

The Amplified Old Testament, Part 2, Copyright © 1964 by Zondervan Publishing House. Used by Permission.

WHY I WROTE THIS BOOK

Ever since I wrote the book **666,** a novel on the Tribulation Period, I felt compelled to finish writing on God's complete panorama of prophecy.

The logical follow-up would be a book on the 1000 year Millennial Age since this period comes after the 7 year Tribulation Period.

And that's what troubled me! The little research I had done through the years on the Millennium convinced me...that while it was a period of unsurpassed blessings...there was not much available detail on this in Scriptures that could fill a novel.

I had accepted Christ as my personal Saviour at 8 years of age at Montrose Bible Conference in Montrose, Pennsylvania.

As I recalled the many, many years I sat under Bible teaching and preaching, I could not recall ever hearing a message on the Millennium. I am sure that there have been messages given on this portion of Bible truth, but my impression is that they are few and far between.

This amazed me.

The Millennium...a period where believers will spend 1000 years! And yet very little is said about it from our pulpits.

This, in part, convinced me that perhaps there wasn't much to say about the Millennium.

But my heart would not give me an inner peace. The Lord was telling me to write a book on the 1000 years. And I knew I would not have peace until I did so.

I began to personally search the Scriptures...reading all available books on the subject...checking and cross-checking.

This would not be an easy book to write. It would be like building a house. I would have to map out a very extensive blueprint of what the Millennium is, its blessings, its government, its activities, and its participants.

Hours and hours of research were finally condensed into 11 pages of framework.

Finally I was ready to write the book. I felt the form of a novel would best explain all the details Scripture tells us about this 1000 year Millennium Period.

This would not be a novel in the ordinary sense of the word. Events and characters would have to be plausable...and the sequence of events and the events themselves must dovetail into what God tells us about the Millennium. This took careful weaving of the fabric of the story line.

Author finishing last chapter of book **1000**.

The book has ten chapters. Actually, the research and the building of an 11-page framework took more time than the writing of the book!

Before I began each chapter I asked the Lord for guidance, clarity of mind and fluidity of thought. He answered my prayers.

Following the pattern of **666,** I believed it very important that Bible references be included right in the paragraphs to which they pertain.

While this is a novel, and the characters are fictitious, it is important to remember that the framework of the book is anchored in biblical FACT.

There WILL BE a 1000 year Millennium Period.

There WILL BE a Judgment, just prior to this period, of the Nation Israel.

There WILL BE a Judgment also of the Gentiles.

There WILL BE great social and economic changes.

Satan WILL BE bound in the bottomless pit during this 1000 years and then be released at the end of this period for a brief time.

God WILL reign during this 1000 years in a Theocratic government whose headquarters will be in Jerusalem!

May I suggest you read THE SEQUENCE OF EVENTS (on succeeding pages) which gives you a bird's-eye view of the entire Millennial Age on which the book **1000** was based.

May I make one more suggestion.

The book **1000** was NOT written to entertain. Undoubtedly many who read this book will consider it an interesting science-fiction story. IT IS NOT!

This book deals with LIFE and DEATH.

Your life...or your death!

You have a life span of only some 70 years here on earth.

You have a life span of an eternity...after death...

either resurrected with Christ
to spend an eternity in Heaven

or

resurrected to meet Christ as your Judge
at the Great White Throne Judgment
and condemned
   to spend an eternity in the Lake of Fire!
                              (Revelation 20:11-15)

Where should your priorities lie? With this present life or making sure of your final destination in a life where you will spend all of eternity!

In the presence of eternity, the mountains are as transient as the clouds.

It was Daniel Defoe who wrote back in 1701:

Wherever God erects a house of prayer,
The Devil always builds a chapel there;
And 'twill be found, upon examination,
The latter has the largest congregation.

Before you read **1000**...determine to read it as though you are actually playing a part in this Millennium Period.

After reading the book, if you find your own beliefs (or lack of them) places you in the congregation of the damned...then chapter 10 can be the most important chapter in your life. And it can point you to life.

My prayer is that you might choose life!

That's why I wrote this book!

Salem Kirban
Huntingdon Valley, Pennsylvania
April, 1973

THE COMING SEQUENCE OF EVENTS
in GOD'S PROPHETIC TIMETABLE

The sequence of events, according to God's Word, the Bible, appears to be as follows:

RAPTURE, including the FIRST RESURRECTION

This can occur at any time. Believing Christians (both dead and alive) will "in the twinkling of an eye" rise up to meet Christ in the air. Read 1 Thessalonians 4:13-17 and Revelation 20.

TRIBULATION

This will be a period of 7 years, following the Rapture, of phenomenal world trial and suffering. It is at this time that Antichrist will reign over a federation of 10 nations which quite possibly could include the United States. See Daniel 9:27 and Matthew 24:21.

*BATTLE of ARMAGEDDON

This will occur at the end of the 7 year Tribulation Period when the Lord Jesus Christ comes down from Heaven and wipes out the combined armies of more than 200 million men. The blood bath covers over 185 miles of Israel. See Revelation 14:20, and 19:11-21.

(While there is a 7 year period of Tribulation on earth... believers, who have already been raptured into heaven, will stand before their Lord to receive crowns and rewards. Their sins have already been paid for at the cross. See 2 Corinthians 5:10. This is called the **JUDGMENT SEAT OF CHRIST**).

*JUDGMENT of the NATION ISRAEL

Before the 1000 year Millennium begins all **living** Israel will be regathered in Palestine (Ezekiel 20:35). The unbelievers will be cut off (Ezekiel 20:37) and cast into Hades, and eventually into the Lake of Fire (Matthew 25:30). The believers, those who have accepted Jesus Christ as Messiah and Lord, will be taken into the Millennium (Ezekiel 20:40-44).

*JUDGMENT of the GENTILES

Before the 1000 year Millennium but after the Judgment of the Nation Israel...all **living** Gentiles who have survived the Tribulation Period will be regathered in Jerusalem (Joel 3:2; Zechariah 14:4). The unbelievers will be cast into Hades, and eventually into the Lake of Fire (Matthew 25: 41). The believers, those who have accepted Jesus Christ as Saviour and Lord, will live on earth for the Millennium Period (Matthew 25:34).

*RESURRECTION of the TRIBULATION SAINTS

Those who have accepted Christ during the Tribulation Period will be raised from the dead by the close of the Tribulation's 7 years as part of the First Resurrection (Daniel 12:1-2 and Revelation 20).

*DISPOSITION OF EVIL ONES

During this same period...at the end of the Tribulation... Antichrist and the False Prophet are thrown into the Lake of Fire (Revelation 19:20).

Satan is bound in the bottomless pit for 1000 years (Revelation 20:1-3).

*MILLENNIUM (1000 Years) REIGN OF CHRIST

This is a period when all the believers of all the ages reign with Christ. Those previously resurrected in the Rapture and those saints who died in the Tribulation and were *resurrected*...will reign with Christ in the Millennial Age as **Resurrected believers.** They will be given positions of responsibility in the Millennial Kingdom (Matthew 19:28, Luke 19:12-27).

The saved of Israel will again be in a position of prominence (Isaiah 49:22-23). They will be given positions of leadership (Isaiah 61:5-6). Gentiles and Jews alike who are still *living* at the close of the Battle of Armageddon, and who are permitted to enter the Millennial Kingdom, are known as **Living Believers.** These were not raptured (they were not believers at the time of the Rapture), nor did they die in the Tribulation period (they survived). They are still in their human unresurrected bodies.

During the Millennium these **Living Believers** will still be able to reproduce children. Children born of these Living Believers will still be born with a sin nature. And for them, salvation is still required. They must individually make a decision whether to accept Jesus Christ as Saviour and Lord...or to deny Him (Ezekiel 36:37-38; Jeremiah 30:19-20).

*THE FINAL REBELLION

At the end of the 1000 year Millennium Period, Satan will have a brief and last opportunity to deceive people. You must remember that many will be born during the Millennial Period. Millions will follow Satan. This vast number of people will completely encircle the Living Believers within Jerusalem in a state of siege.

When this occurs, God brings fire down from Heaven killing the millions of Satan's army (Revelation 20).

*GREAT WHITE THRONE JUDGMENT

This is when the unsaved, non-believers, of all of the ages are resurrected and are judged before God. These are condemned forever to the Lake of Fire. Both living (from the Millennium) and dead **unsaved** are judged here. Those previously dead, up to this point, have already been in hell in torment, awaiting this Final Judgment Day (Revelation 20:11-15).

EARTH BURNS UP

To purify this earth, so tainted with the scars of sin, God sets it afire with a fervent heat. See 2 Peter 3:7,10.

The NEW HEAVENS and the NEW EARTH

All Christians finally reach the ultimate in glory reigning forever with Christ in a new heaven and a new earth (Revelation 21).

*Those time periods preceded by an asterisk (*) are the area that the novel **1000** covers. If you give special attention to these portions of God's Plan for tomorrow, you will understand the book **1000** much better.

Chapter 1 of the book **1000** begins with the final stages of the BATTLE OF ARMAGEDDON.

(Anyone interested in a detailed examination of why these events are placed in this order, etc., may refer to J. Dwight Pentecost's large reference book, *Things to Come;* Grand Rapids: Zondervan Publishing Co., 1958. See pages 370-546.)

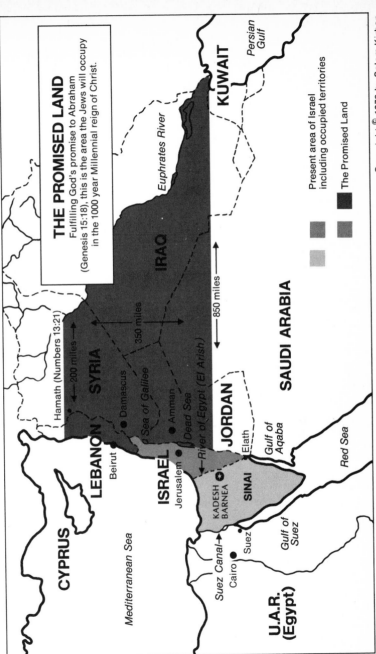

THE PROMISED LAND

Fulfilling God's promise to Abraham (Genesis 15:18), this is the area the Jews will occupy in the 1000 year Millennial reign of Christ.

Present area of Israel including occupied territories

The Promised Land

Copyright © 1973 by Salem Kirban

CYPRUS

Mediterranean Sea

LEBANON

Beirut

ISRAEL

Jerusalem

KADESH BARNEA

SINAI

Suez Canal

Cairo

Suez

Gulf of Suez

U.A.R. (Egypt)

Red Sea

Gulf of Aqaba

Elath

JORDAN

River of Egypt (El Arish)

Dead Sea

Amman

Sea of Galilee

Damascus

SYRIA

Hamath (Numbers 13:21)

200 miles

350 miles

850 miles

IRAQ

Euphrates River

KUWAIT

Persian Gulf

SAUDI ARABIA

IN EXPLANATION

While this book...**1000**
deals with the conflicts
>   just prior to the Millennium
>   and in the Millennium itself,

Believers
>   (those who have accepted Christ as
>   Lord and Saviour)

**should realize that for them it will be 1000 years of
almost perfect happiness and contentment.**

WHAT AN INHERITANCE!

All of the wonderful things which man has vainly sought in his own strength, without God, will at last be poured out in the Kingdom of His Son during the 1000 year MILLENNIUM.

With Satan imprisoned during this time (Revelation 20:1-7) . . . the Millennium Period will be one of

1. PEACE

     Because there will be no war, nations will not have to devote a great part of their budget to war materials. There will be an economic prosperity such as never before has been experienced.

     (Isaiah 11:6-9)

     Perhaps the most well-known verse in relation to this is:
     "And He shall judge between the nations, and shall decide (disputes) for many people; and they shall beat their swords into plowshares, and their spears into pruning hooks; nation shall not lift up sword against nation, neither shall they learn war any more."

     (Isaiah 2:4 Amplified Bible)

Many political leaders use this verse referring to the goals of this present world. However, this verse refers to the coming MILLENNIUM 1000 YEAR AGE . . . not to this present age.

2. HAPPINESS
This will be the fulfillment of happiness because there will be no more war nor will there be the multitude of sorrows now present to man on this earth.
(Revelation 20:3; Isaiah 11:6-9)

"Therefore with joy will you draw water from the wells of salvation."
(Isaiah 12:3 Amplified Bible)

3. LONG LIFE AND HEALTH
Here in the 1000 year Millennial Period both sickness and death will be well nigh removed. Death will not be banished completely, however, during this period. Open sin may cause some to die because the Millennial Period, while filled with multiple blessings is still not the end of God's final judgments.
(Isaiah 65:20)

Keep these things in mind, however:
A. The DEFORMED will be HEALED
"And in that day shall the deaf hear the words of the book, and out of obscurity and gloom and darkness the eyes of the blind shall see."
(Isaiah 29:18 Amplified Bible; also read Isaiah 35:5,6)
B. SICKNESS will be REMOVED
"And no inhabitant will say, I am sick. . . ."
(Isaiah 33:24 Amplified Bible)
C. SEXUAL REPRODUCTION will EXIST
Those saints who live through the Tribulation Period and enter the 1000 MILLENNIUM in their natural bodies will be able to have children throughout this 1000 year age. In fact the population of the earth will once again become great.
But it must be kept in mind that those who are born DURING the 1000 year Millennial Age will have a sin nature and it WILL be necessary for them to accept Christ if they are to participate in the final and continuing eternity that begins after this 1000 year period.

Here are two more verses to help you understand this wonderful blessing:

> "Out of them shall come songs of thanksgiving and the voices of those who make merry. And I will multiply them, and they shall not be few; I will also glorify them, and they shall not be small."

> "Their children too shall be as in former times. . . ."
> *(Jeremiah 30:19,20 Amplified Bible)*

4. PROSPERITY

The Millennium Period will be one of unequalled prosperity. There will be such an abundance that there will be no want.

Perhaps the most familiar verse . . . and one we hear quoted as only beginning to come to pass today . . . is the verse below, which actually refers to the 1000 year MILLENNIUM PERIOD:

> "The wilderness and the dry land shall be glad, the desert shall rejoice and blossom as the rose and the autumn crocus.
> It shall blossom abundantly, and rejoice even with joy and singing; the glory of Lebanon shall be given to it, the excellency of Mount Carmel and the plain of Sharon. . . ."
> *(Isaiah 35:1,2 Amplified Bible)*

Think about this for a moment!

Here will be a desert that will have all the *glory of Lebanon* given to it! The glory of Lebanon is found in the strength and stateliness of its cedars. *The excellency of Carmel and Sharon,* which consisted of corn and cattle, will likewise then characterize this transformed desert!

5. A JOY IN LABOR

Under the direction of Christ there will be a perfect economic system in which people will work in complete joy and desire to provide the necessities of life.

> "They shall build houses and inhabit them, and they shall plant vineyards and eat the fruit of them . . . My chosen and elect shall long make use of and enjoy the work of their hands."
> *(Isaiah 65:21,22 Amplified Bible)*

6. LANGUAGE WILL BE PURE

In this blessed period language will not be used for taking God's name in vain or for other wrong purposes. Lips will glorify and praise God. Perhaps the language of the earth will at this time be unified.

"For then I will give to the people a clear and pure speech from pure lips . . ."

(Zephaniah 3:9 Amplified Bible)

7. GOD WILL BE PRESENT

This will be a time when we can fellowship with God and enjoy His manifested presence in a special way.

"My tabernacle or dwelling place also shall be with them; and I will be their God. . . ."

"The abode of God is with men, and He will live among them, and they shall be His people and God shall personally be with them and be their God."

(Ezekiel 37:27, Revelation 21:3 Amplified Bible)

While much of this book. . .**1000,** deals with the conflicts of the early days immediately following the Tribulation, the reader should remember that the vast majority of the time of the Millennium (hundreds of years) will be filled with an abundance of prosperity, happiness and international goodwill.

There will be virtually no sickness, no poverty, no death. The limited exceptions are incorporated in this book. . .**1000.**

The greatest battle this world will ever experience and the largest casualty rate in history will occur at the end of the 1000 Millennium Period when Satan is loosed for a brief period of time.

With this background information in mind you should be able to read the novel **1000** with greater understanding.

Salem Kirban

3 DECISIVE WARS

War	Participants	Occurs	Reason for War	Outcome	Scripture References
	Russia and Allies (Arab nations, Iran, Germany) vs. Israel	Before or during first 3½ years of Tribulation Period (This could happen at any time!)	Russia desires Israel's vast mineral wealth.	God will intervene and through an earthquake in Israel plus rain and hail, the Russian army will be wiped out. It will take the Israelites 7 years to collect the debris. It will also take them 7 months to bury the dead!	Ezekiel 38:1-39:16
Battle of Armageddon	Armies from All Nations vs. God at Jerusalem	At End of 7 year Tribulation Period	Flushed with power Antichrist will defy God, seek to destroy the 144,000 witnessing Jews and Jerusalem.	The Lord Jesus Christ comes down from heaven and wipes out the combined armies of more than 200 million men. The blood bath covers over 185 miles of Israel and is "even unto the horse bridles." (Revelation 14:20) Antichrist and the False Prophet are cast alive into the Lake of Fire. (Revelation 19:20) Satan is bound in the bottomless pit for 1000 years. (Revelation 20:1-3)	Joel 3:9, 12 Zechariah 14:1-4 Revelation 16:13-16 Revelation 19:11-21 Ezekiel 39:17-29
The Final Rebellion	Satan vs. God	At End of 1000 year Millennium Period	God allows Satan one more opportunity on earth to preach his deceiving message.	Satan will be successful in deceiving vast multitudes (out of those born during the millennial period) to turn away from Christ. This horde of perhaps millions of people will completely circle the Believers in Jerusalem in a state of siege. When this occurs, God brings FIRE down from Heaven killing the millions in Satan's army. Satan is then cast into the Lake of Fire, where the False Prophet and Antichrist are, and they will be tormented day and night for ever and ever.	Revelation 20:7-10

Chapter 1

THE GREAT REUNION

What he saw seemed like a dream. Could it be true? Or would he suddenly wake up into reality?

After struggling through seven long years for survival...against what seemed to be incredible odds...victory seemed impossible.

And George Omega was crying. Imagine, he a grown man...crying.

But George Omega could not hold back the tears.

A hardened newspaperman who had witnessed and reported on many tragedies...a man who had seen death first hand...had related stories of man's inhumanity to man...had come to accept both the joys and the tragedies as "matter of fact." As anchorman for the World Television Network...he had once been respected...but these last seven years he was hunted. And the hunter was Brother Bartholomew, President of the United States of Europe.

Now it was all over. No more running.

Suddenly the reality of it all hit him...like a blast of cold air refreshing a steamy desert.

And he cried!

With tears streaming down his rugged face...he turned to Faye Sanders, his daughter...

"Faye, it's over. It's over. Praise God...every promise of the Bible IS true!"

"Daddy, you're crying. And I'm so happy, too. Daddy, the King is here...and NOTHING WILL EVER BE THE SAME AGAIN!"

I remembered the many times I had arrived home by plane and searched the crowds for my wife, Helen.

And she was never there. I had never understood the Rapture. The sea of faces brought me quickly to reality. It was then that I had realized that not only Helen but also our two children, Sue and Tommy, no longer lived on earth. I feared that this separation would be eternal. And that would be a long time.

> And it shall be said in that day, Lo, this is our God; we have waited for Him, and He will save us: this is the Lord; we have waited for Him, we will be glad and rejoice in His salvation.
>
> (Isaiah 25:9)

How often I had remembered quoting from *Antony and Cleopatra* the familiar line:

"Eternity was in our lips and eyes."

And Helen would burst into tears...hold me tightly (as though in the mere holding she could snatch me from an eternity of separation).

I'll never forget the look of love in her eyes as she would softly quote a poem she had written which she called her "poem of love."

Even now I could still hear her voice:

> Eternity is not a moment's tears
> For those who turn away
> Eternity is endless years
> A night with no more day!

Helen knew me better than I knew myself. And somehow I guess she knew that I would never make it at the Rapture. I got the feeling that she was preparing me for what was ahead. And each time she came to that second verse, she would clutch me close to her, look up into my eyes, softly kiss me, and as the tears came tumbling down her cheeks, repeat:

Eternity is not a moment's love
For those who seek His light
Eternity is Heaven above
A day with no more night!

I was so overcome with emotion...I whispered these last lines into Faye's ear.

"Think of it, Faye, it's here...a day with no more night."

I was referring to the fact that soon Helen and our family and Bill Sanders, Faye's husband, would all be together again.

Little did I realize the significance of that statement.

And that's why I was crying!

The heavens had opened. Suddenly the dark clouds disappeared. It was like taking off on a rainy, gloomy day and suddenly breaking through the cloud barrier into brilliant sunlight.

Our days of stumbling in darkness, in defeat, in despair were over. Suddenly it was as though over the entire earth a heavenly light had been switched on. Darkness had simply disappeared ...vanished. Everything was light.

Faye and I searched the sea of faces coming down from the Heavens. I can remember the first time I saw man actually land on the moon. It just seemed unbelievable.

And this scene was even more unbelievable. There...actually coming down from the Heavens was Jesus Christ...actually riding on a white horse...and there riding with Him were the troops of Heaven. It was a scene of joy for Faye and me...but the very countenance of Christ was one of judgment.

...justice is far from us, and righteousness does not overtake us; We hope for light, but behold, darkness; For brightness, but we walk in gloom.

We grope along the wall like blind men, We grope like those who have no eyes; We stumble at midday as in the twilight, Among those who are vigorous we are like dead men.

(Isaiah 59:9-10 ASV)

For it will be a unique day which is known to the Lord, neither day nor night; but it will come about that at evening time there will be light.

(Zechariah 14:7 ASV)

There...actually coming down from the Heavens was Jesus Christ...and riding with Him were the troops of Heaven.

It was then that I caught a familiar face. After years of searching the crowds at airports ...now in the sky, I could see Helen, Sue, Tommy and Bill... and even Tom Malone who had saved my life a short time ago... at the expense of his.

Faye was jumping up and down for joy. "Daddy, look there's Bill! And look, over there, it's little Sue with Tommy. But, Daddy, they're no longer small. What happened? Why they've grown up!"

"Faye, there's a lot we don't know right now...but soon it will all be made clear. I haven't seen them for years...and yet we recognize them. Faye, I'm so happy."

And I saw heaven opened, and behold a white horse; and He that sat upon him was called Faithful and True, and in righteousness He doth judge and make war.

His eyes were as a flame of fire, and on His head were many crowns; and He had a name written that no man knew, but He Himself.

And He was clothed with a vesture dipped in blood: and His name is called The Word of God.

And the armies which were in heaven followed Him upon white horses, clothed in fine linen, white and clean.

And out of His mouth goeth a sharp sword, that with it He should smite the nations: and He shall rule them with a rod of iron: and He treadeth the winepress of the fierceness and wrath of Almighty God.

(Revelation 19:11-15)

"Daddy, how will I talk to them? Will their bodies be like mine? Will they recognize us? Will we be married? Will Bill still be my husband?"

"Faye, easy now, I'm just as confused as you. I could kick myself for not reading up on Bible prophecy. And now, I just don't have the answers. Come to think of it, I can remember Helen saying she had never heard anyone preach on the Millennium."

"Millennium? What's that Daddy?"

"Millennium means *1000 years,* Faye. That's one thing I remember. After the 7 years of Tribulation...which we just went through...comes this 1000 years."

"But why wouldn't anyone preach about it, Daddy?"

"Oh, I suppose some ministers have...but Helen never heard a message on it. I remember in those Last Days before Helen was raptured...the few times I did go to church...seems to me the big theme was love. I got the feeling they believed love would cure everything. Their hypocrisy sickened me...they spent more money on building large churches and selling everyone on bigger and bigger congregations...so much so they never had time to pray for little Mrs. Smith who was sick...or old Mr. Jones...that is, unless he had money."

"Did Mom ever mention hearing anything about the future age?"

"Yes, Faye, she attended a church where prophecy was preached quite regularly...so much so that the man was labeled a sensationalist. But I don't recall her saying that even he preached on the Millennium."

"Guess he just couldn't understand it, Daddy."

"Guess not, I know I don't. But we know it's real, Faye... because it's here...RIGHT NOW!"

* * *

Sylvia Caraway had tasted of every luxury. She had considered herself fortunate. "Marry a rich Jewish man," her mother told her, "they treat their wives well, and life will be a bed of roses."

For a while it proved more than that...it was a bed of orchids.

And Sylvia loved every minute of it...or at least she thought so.

Sylvia had grown up in the tenement row houses of Brooklyn. Poverty—she had plenty of it. Everday was potato soup. She got her greatest childhood thrills by joining her friends in smashing school windows, jamming typewriter keys, and setting schools on fire. One day she read where the city of New York spent $1 million just replacing school windows. It thrilled her to know she had a part in this carnage.

At the age of 14 she had experienced every known thrill. And from that day on she set her sights on marrying a millionaire.

Then one day she met Abel...and she knew that this was her man.

Abel Epstein had a corner on the teen magazines and record

publishing business. Everything his hand touched seemed to turn to gold.

When they were married in Palm Springs...Abel gave her a $25,000 Rolls-Royce. Nothing was too good for her. "Sylvia," he would say, "your bed of orchids is made possible by the teenage bubblegum set."

Abel gave her a $25,000 Rolls-Royce. Nothing was too good for her.

Then he would go on to explain how he and others made millions on record promotions. He told me that in 1971 the Osmond Brothers, David Cassidy, the Jackson Five and a couple others collected royalties on more than $60 million worth of nonrecord merchandise alone...shirts, posters and the like.

But this was too easy for Abel...and soon he was tinkering in experiments with light. That's how he got involved in the Laser Beam market.

"Sylvia," he said one day, "I always did like the impossible and I think I've latched on to a moneymaker."

I'll never forget, Sylvia recalled to herself, the day Abel finally came up with a winner—the Laser Ring.

Somehow I was frightened when one day we were visited by

Brother Bartholomew. Why was he so interested in this discovery? Why did he make Abel feel so important...important enough to offer him a post in government.

That's all Abel needed.

"Sylvia, I've reached the top. For once in my life, I'm really important."

I questioned that.

"Important for what, Abel, because your new invention can kill masses quickly? Have you so easily forgotten your own people and what Hitler did to them in Germany?"

"Don't talk foolish, Sylvia. We're living in an enlightened age. Brother Bartholomew assures me this Laser Ring will be used in the pursuit of peace."

Somehow, I couldn't believe him. But once Abel made up his mind...no one changed it. He gave me plenty of money. So why worry? For me the life to live would be continuous luxury. But somehow, worry I did.

Within a short time we flew to Jerusalem. "That's where all the action is," Abel kept telling me. And action there was. It was to change my life.

It was there I came across a book that at first appeared to me to be science-fiction.

It told about the Tribulation Period of 7 years...about a rising man of peace who would become a man of terror. Then it all came back to me. My early childhood years...church... those Sundays when I put off accepting Christ as my Saviour. Then my life had more than ever become filled with sin and greed.

But there in Jerusalem amid those awful tribulation period years, I at last repented and turned to Christ as my Saviour. The glow of the world had suddenly lost its luster. For the first time in my life I found real abiding peace, and the riches that surrounded me seemed like filthy rags.

I wanted to tell my new-found discovery to someone but I knew Abel would laugh in my face. I can still hear him now, "Don't

But we are all as an unclean thing, and all our righteousnesses are as filthy rags; and we all do fade as a leaf; and our iniquities, like the wind, have taken us away. (Isaiah 64:6)

tell me Sylvia's got religion.
Your religion is in your mink coat, your Rolls-Royce, your
jet-set friends, your houseful of servants...come on baby...
don't spoil it for us...live it up."

Whatever I would say would simply fall on deaf ears. And
each time I did try to witness to him of the tragedy that would
befall him...he would laugh all the harder.

"Sylvia, you've got some imagination. You ought to write a
novel. Who ever heard of God coming down from the sky...and
on a horse at that...and all those so-called Christians that died
...riding on white horses. What a laugh. Why 99% of those
people never rode a horse in their life...let alone riding a
horse some 10,000 feet in the air. Won't that be a sight!"

I knew it was useless. It would have been easier fabricating
a lie...something really out in left field.

"Hell? Sylvia there is no hell and no heaven. Hell is here on
earth. I worked hard for my money. That's heaven. And let
me cut you off without one red cent. And you'll find that's
hell!"

That was the final straw. Tears came to my eyes. Abel had
been so thoroughly brainwashed. He was already believing a
lie! It was like a cancer that was eating within him. And
nothing I could say would change his mind.

Do you know what it is to
stumble across some good news
...and have no one to share it
with? That's how I felt. Abel
wouldn't listen, and his friends

**And for this cause God shall
send them strong delusion, that
they should believe a lie.**
(2 Thessalonians 2:11)

were equally as deaf to the impending tragedy.

That's when I thought of Terry Malone. She knew what suffering was all about. Her husband Tom had been Presidential
Secretary to Brother Bartholomew. And it was Abel's cruel
invention, the Ruby Laser, that had snuffed out Tom's life a
short time ago...a death ray directed from the sinister hand of
Brother Bartholomew.

But Terry had acted strangely lately. Up until a few days ago she was always telling me about Christ. In whispered tones she often urged me to decide now for Christ...unravelling the panorama of events that was to happen. And while I found her story fantastic, her warmth and dedication impressed me. I knew I could turn to her in a time of stress.

But now, it appeared as though a shadow had crossed her path. And when I rushed to tell her the good news...that Terry Malone's Saviour was my Saviour, too...there was a veiled happiness on her face.

I knew that since Tom's death she had been on Brother Bartholomew's social calendar. Rumors had it that BB (as we called him) had made a secret visit to her home when Tom ran off with George Omega and his daughter, Faye Sanders. That's when Tom was blasted into eternity by the Ruby Laser.

"Terry," I said, "I thought you'd be the happiest person in the world when I told you the good news that I'm in Christ now ...I have no more fears...why even my desire for easy living and wealth are gone...I wouldn't even mind scrubbing floors. Terry, when you hear me say that...you know it's for real."

Terry in a half-hearted smile replied: "I am glad, Sylvia, very glad. It's just that...oh, never mind...you would never understand. Please forgive me."

Suddenly the sky lit up. Such brightness I had never seen. I knew something was about to happen.

And my only regret was that Terry was not sharing in that joy.

* * *

Abel Epstein had reached the top. Right there at Megiddo he was helping Brother Bartholomew in the movement of armies on that vast plain.

"I think we have those Chinese licked, sir. It's just hard to tell, the clouds are obstructing my view."

A grin of smug satisfaction wreathed his face as he thought, "Wait till I tell Sylvia how we licked that Chinese Army of 200 million men...me and BB. Bet I'll become Presidential Adviser after this."

"Sir," Epstein directed his comments to Brother Bartholomew, "looks like Israel is going to be ours. Reports indicate that Jerusalem has just about had it!"

"Glad to hear that Abel. With Jerusalem falling, the whole world will be ours. This puts you in line for a promotion, too. Now the world will know who to believe in. Those Bible prophets swayed too many of our people. We'll set them straight."

For thus saith the Lord of hosts; After the glory hath He sent me unto the nations which spoiled you: for he that toucheth you toucheth the apple of His eye.

(Zechariah 2:8)

Nothing could have made Abel happier. In his record selling days he was known as a wheeler and dealer. He knew all the angles. He prided himself in the fact that he could "sell refrigerators in Alaska." In no way would he miss out on this victory. And, if Sylvia, was right and there was a Heaven and Hell...

And in that day will I make Jerusalem a burdensome stone for all people: all that burden themselves with it shall be cut in pieces, though all the people of the earth be gathered together against it.

And it shall come to pass in that day, that I will seek to destroy all the nations that come against Jerusalem.

(Zechariah 12:3,9)

he'd deal himself right into Heaven too.

Suddenly it seemed as if the world stood still.

The heavens opened.

He gasped in amazement as he looked into the sky. There were those horses...with riders. The leader appeared to have eyes of penetrating fire.

Reports were jamming Brother Bartholomew's control tower of operations.

"Our armored cavalrymen are going blind, sir. They appear disoriented."

"Get the officers to keep them in check," BB bellowed.

"Can't sir, even the officers seem berserk...like they're going mad. Advise instructions. I can't control the army any longer but ...."

In that day, says the Lord, I will smite every horse [of the armies that contend against Jerusalem] with terror and panic, and his rider with madness; and I will open My eyes and regard with favor the house of Judah, and will smite every horse of the opposing nations with blindness.

(Zechariah 12:4 Amplified Bible)

Abel Epstein quickly turned on all orbiting TV stations. The entire wall in front of him was a panel of pictures. The carnage of death that filled the screens was unbelievable!

With that came sudden silence as though his sentence had been cut short even before completion.

Abel Epstein quickly turned on all orbiting TV stations. The entire wall in front of him was a panel of pictures...each showing a portion of the plains that lie before them.

> Now this will be the plague with which the Lord will strike all the peoples who have gone to war against Jerusalem; their flesh will rot while they stand on their feet, and their eyes will rot in their sockets, and their tongue will rot in their mouth.
> (Zechariah 14:12 ASV)

The carnage of death that filled the screens was unbelievable... and everywhere there appeared to be thousands of blind soldiers being trampled on by stampeding men, vehicles, and horses.

Suddenly a staggering light pierced the sanctity of BB's control center.

> And he shall plant the tabernacles of his palace between the seas in the glorious holy mountain; yet he shall come to his end, and none shall help him.
> (Daniel 11:45)

Abel Epstein blinked his eyes... turned around...but Brother Bartholomew had vanished!

* * *

To Faye and George it was like having a box seat at the Inauguration of a President.

Standing on the Mount of Olives they had witnessed the flash of light that suddenly struck in the direction of Megiddo. At that time they did not realize that Brother Bartholomew had quickly met his end and was now in the Lake of Fire.

Both Faye and George knew that reunion with their loved ones would soon be accomplished.

> And the beast [Antichrist] was taken, and with him the false prophet that wrought miracles before him, with which he deceived them that had received the mark of the beast, and them that worshipped his image. These both were cast alive into a lake of fire burning with brimstone. (Revelation 19:20)

"Daddy, what will it be like? Will I be able to touch mom and talk to her? Will I be able to kiss Bill...just like when we first met?"

Then the reality of all those years struck home. All they had yearned for was about to happen.

Would it be too much for them?

It was a time when they should be filled with joy...yet, there was some apprehension.

"I just don't know, Faye, I just don't know. Helen, Sue and Tommy and Bill and even Tom Malone will have new bodies. We do know that. They will be real bodies of flesh and bones. But they will be resurrected bodies...like a glorious continuation of our present bodies."

"But I just don't understand," Faye interrupted.

"I know it's hard honey, but you understand the caterpillar, don't you? Remember when you used to catch one when you were small. I would find you a jar and punch a couple holes in the lid. You put in a few twigs and some leaves. Then one day, what happened?"

"The caterpillar disappeared! I mean it went into a cocoon it had spun for itself."

"That's right, Faye...a cocoon ...like a casket. If you had opened it, it would appear lifeless and without much form. But then, remember the day you ran downstairs from the bedroom shouting for me to come up. And when we looked...there in that bottle was a beautiful butterfly with brilliant wings. Did we keep it in the bottle?"

...some will say, "How are the dead raised? And with what kind of body do they come?"

You fool! That which you sow does not come to life unless it dies;

And that which you sow, you do not sow the body which is to be, but a bare grain, perhaps of wheat or of something else.

But God gives it a body just as He wished, and to each of the seeds a body of its own.
(1 Corinthians 15:35-38 ASV)

"No, dad, we let it fly out in the open skies and in the sunshine."

"Faye, I think that was one of God's object lessons to us on how our resurrected bodies will come forth in new beauty. We don't understand it. But we know it is a reality."

"Will we have the same habits, Daddy? And what about Bill. Will he still be his same old stubborn self?"

"No, Faye, when we meet them everything will change. You will see."

So also is the resurrection of the dead. It is sown in corruption; it is raised in incorruption.

It is sown a natural body; it is raised a spiritual body. There is a natural body, and there is a spiritual body.
(1 Corinthians 15:42,44)

"Will they be able to walk through doors like Jesus did when He met the disciples after His resurrection?"

> It is sown in dishonour; it is raised in glory: it is sown in weakness; it is raised in power.
> (1 Corinthians 15:43)

"We soon will see, Faye. After all if we can accept x-rays and radio waves that penetrate bodies and walls...why should it be any more difficult to accept the fact that resurrected bodies can do the same or more. In Christ we will be liberated from physical and earthly restraints."

"It seems fantastic Dad. Won't it be great to see Mom and Bill and everyone. It's been so long. And we can recognize them, can't we, Dad?"

> For if we believe that Jesus died and rose again, even so them also which sleep in Jesus will God bring with Him.
> (1 Thessalonians 4:14)

"Of course, honey, Moses and Elijah were recognized on the Mount of Transfiguration. The risen Lord was known to His disciples and to Mary at the tomb."

Just then, a swoosh of air seemed to engulf them.

Faye and George looked around.

There, next to them, on the Mount of Olives was Helen, Sue, Tommy, and Faye's husband, Bill Sanders.

Faye and George were overwhelmed with joy. Bill still had his dimples. Sue and Tommy were mature young adults. There were no more tears of separation as Helen whispered tenderly into George's ear, "Sweetheart, I missed you at the Rapture...but it's all over now...and we're together again."

For Bill and Faye it was a tender moment. Bill, who just a short time ago had died under

> ...He took Peter and John and James, and went up into a mountain to pray... And, behold, there talked with Him two men, which were Moses and Elijah.... (Luke 9:28,30)
>
> * * *
>
> And as they thus spake, Jesus Himself stood in the midst of them... and He said... Behold my hands and my feet, that it is I myself: handle me, and see; for a spirit hath not flesh and bones, as ye see me have.
>
> (Luke 34:36,39)
>
> * * *
>
> Jesus saith unto her, Woman, why seekest thou? whom seekest thou? She, supposing Him to be the gardener, saith unto Him, Sir, if thou have borne Him hence, tell me where thou hast laid Him, and I will take Him away.
>
> Jesus saith unto her, Mary. She turned herself, and saith unto Him, Rabboni; which is to say, Master. (John 20:15-16)

the blade of a guillotine, was now in Faye's arms...perfect and whole in a completed resurrected body. It was a great reunion!

* * *

Just a few feet away Sylvia placed her arm about Terry Malone. And then witnessing the phenomenon in the sky... suddenly released her grip. Within a moment Tom Malone was there...beaming as he whirled Terry in his arms.

And for Terry Malone the great reunion was filled with happiness, but beyond the outer joy Sylvia sensed a heart burdened with tears!

Chapter 2

SORROW at SINAI

Abel Epstein was both bewildered and furious. Where had Brother Bartholomew disappeared? And what a time to leave!

Every phone in the control center was ringing. And each one he answered brought messages of utter confusion and calamity.

"Get us help, get us help. Mayday! Mayday! Some unseen force is wiping out our entire army!"

Abel Epstein, in an attempt to remain calm replied, "Pull back your forces 3 miles and let's reappraise the situation. Brother Bartholomew is not here. He's probably on his way out to the front."

"Negative, sir, he is not here...and we have no forces to pull back. Just the Lieutenant and I remain from our entire regiment."

Epstein angrily slammed down the phone.

For the first time in his life fear suddenly gripped him. Cold sweat poured out over his massive body. He jerked the Jerusalem contact phone from the wall and bellowed, "Get me Dr. Curter."

Dr. Curter was beginning to have doubts about the whole Megiddo expedition as he sat in his laboratory atop Mt. Herzl. From here looking northeast he could see the Mount of Olives.

Picking up his binoculars he scanned the horizon as suddenly the whole area was flooded with brilliant sunlight. Unusual, he thought. Something is happening.

It was only when he spotted Bill Sanders embracing his wife Faye that Dr. Curter lost his composure. His face turned ashen white. How could this be. He had personally witnessed the guillotine execution of Sanders. Could it be a dream?

The jangling phone brought him to his senses.

"Hello, this is Dr. Curter."

"Curter, this is Epstein at Megiddo Control Center. Everyone's gone mad here. Utter chaos. I'm boarding a helicopter. Will be there in 10 minutes. Stay where you are. I have a plan."

"A plan for what?" Dr. Curter was about to ask. But before he could, Epstein had hung up.

As Epstein boarded Brother Bartholomew's helicopter he instructed the pilot to circle the Megiddo plains.

What he saw was unbelievable.

What was once a plain now seemed like a quagmire. Here in the heat of the desert...the dry 105° heat...where in the world did the water come from?

He picked up the radio phone and after several tries finally reached a ground commander.

"What's happening down there? Where's the red mud coming from?"

"It's not mud, sir."

The voice seemed weak.

"Speak up," Epstein demanded.

"I have no strength sir. All around me are bodies...horses and men...and blood...blood... blood. It's...It's like a sea of blood. I can't speak sir...my tongue...I caaaan't...."

And the wine press was trodden outside the city, and blood came out from the wine press, [reaching] as high as horses' bridles, for a distance of one thousand and six hundred stadia [about 200 hundred miles].

(Revelation 14:20
Amplified Bible)

Then it dawned on him. Was what Sylvia had told him finally coming true? No, he couldn't believe such fantastic tales. There

Epstein instructed the pilot to circle the Megiddo plains. What he saw was unbelievable.

had to be an explanation to all of this. The sudden earthquakes ...falling stars...they must have been a chain reaction from the air pollutants. That's it. It can't be God...whoever he is or wherever he is.

The pilot turned to him.

"Sir, if I didn't know better I would say that battlefield looks like a sea of blood...and it looks like it covers miles and miles of the Plain of Esdraelon."

"Nonsense, head this crate for Jerusalem and let's get to Mt. Herzl as quickly as possible."

As Helicopter 1 approached Jerusalem, Epstein's heart sank in despair. He had not been a good Jew but he did remember his early years in Hebrew school... seven years of learning, reading the Talmud.

For, behold, the Lord will come with fire, and with His chariots like a whirlwind, to render His anger with fury, and His rebuke with flames of fire.

For by fire and by His sword will the Lord plead with all flesh: and the slain of the Lord shall be many.

(Isaiah 66:15-16)

He hadn't remembered much. But in the Talmud, Gemarah Kiddushim 496 was a phrase of beauty he had remembered. It was so poetic and so true. As though in prayer he bowed his head and softly repeated it...

> Ten parts of beauty were allotted the world at large: out of these Jerusalem assumed nine measures and the rest of the world but one...
> Ten parts of suffering were visited upon the world — nine for Jerusalem and one for the world.

If there was any tenderness in Epstein's heart...this was the moment. But instead of an awakening towards the Messiah...as he saw the destruction...he became more bitter.

If there is a God, he thought, why did He allow this suffering ...this tragedy to "His" Jerusalem?

"Then he remembered that verse in Psalms...Psalm 137:5-6... and in derision he quoted it:

If I forget you, O Jerusalem,
May my right hand forget her skill
May my tongue cleave to the roof of my mouth,
If I do not remember you,
If I do not exalt Jerusalem
   Above my chief joy.

In his bitterness he thought...the Hebrew school did me some good after all...he remembered that verse. To him it proved that God was not on the scene. For Jerusalem lay waste. The world was upside down.

Abel Epstein, who had come from selling records, to creating a laser ring, was not through yet! He was smarter than God... whoever he was. He, Epstein, would find a way out of this mess. Then he would live it up again!

The sudden descent of the helicopter engine brought him back to reality.

Flying over the Hebrew University the helicopter started its landing pattern onto Mount Herzl.

There was the Hill of Remembrance, on the ridge, dedicated to the six million European Jews killed by the Nazis in World War 2. The sight brought more bitterness to Epstein's heart. "Hitler was a saint compared to Brother Bartholomew," he thought, "why there must be at least 200 million dead out there at Megiddo!"

The helicopter landed atop Mount Herzl. Here Theodore Herzl was buried, the man who was first fired by the vision of a Jewish statehood and launched the movement. In 1949, forty-five years after his death, the body of Dr. Herzl had been brought in state from Vienna to Jerusalem.

The place seemed deserted.

Epstein quickly raced up the marble steps...each step echoing throughout the vast structure. It seemed eerie.

Running down a familiar hall, he came to Dr. Curter's office... swung open the door...and gasped in amazement and fright.

Epstein angrily grabbed a book and hurled it at the bird.

There in the chair was Dr. Curter. He looked alive. But the glassy stare of his eyes revealed differently. What eyes were left. There, perched on his head was a huge bird, gorging his belly as he pecked at Curter's eyes and took chunks from his swollen tongue.

Epstein angrily grabbed a book and hurled it at the bird. The sharp crack was heard throughout the hall as the book squarely hit Dr. Curter's head. His body

And I saw an angel standing in the sun; and he cried with a loud voice, saying to all the fowls that fly in the midst of heaven, Come and gather yourselves together unto the supper of the great God;

That ye may eat the flesh of kings, and the flesh of captains, and the flesh of mighty men, and the flesh of horses, and of them that sit on them, and the flesh of all men, both free and bond, both small and great.

Revelation 19:17-18

slid awkwardly off the chair and sprawled on the floor. As other birds quickly flew in at the smell of open flesh...Epstein ran hysterically from the room and down to the waiting helicopter.

* * *

Sylvia was noticeably worried. Standing there on the Mount of Olives with Terry she could sense something was wrong. Terry should have been overjoyed at this reunion. And she was...but.

Suddenly Sylvia realized in her concern for others and her witnessing this glorious reunion...she had forgotten about herself and Abel.

It was like hitting her with a ton of bricks. "Dear Jesus," she whispered to herself, "I want to be near you...and I want Abel to come to know you as Saviour and Lord."

Funny, she thought. She had thought of Abel as her lucky charm, her security blanket, her ace in the hole. After she married him she never wanted for money, perfume, or furs. Everywhere she went, she went first class. "Baby," he told her, "now that you've married me...you're going to travel first class!"

And first class she went. It was a cold, convenient love. There was never any warmth. Abel was all business in everything he did. He never even took time to eat properly or spend time with her. She was revolted by the way he gulped down a chicken sandwich and a soft drink...then dashed off to another business deal. When she complained, he would reply, "Make up your mind, baby, do you want me or money. You can't have them both."

And for a while, she was glad to settle for the money.

She attended all the social balls in New York. She thought nothing of spending $150 for a ticket to the Diamond Ball at the Plaza and dancing for hours to the bands of Meyer Davis and Peter Duchin.

She remembered even bidding for the Velazquez portrait at Wildenstein Gallery and seemed quite relieved when she was outbid by the final bid of $5.54 million!

Her greatest thrill, or so she thought, was when Abel sent her off on a worldwide cruise aboard the S.S. France. Her cabin cost $99,340 and she remembered filling her cigarette box in her suite with 500 crisp dollar bills for small tips.

And every August, without fail, she would head up to Saratoga Springs, New York for the Saratoga auction of yearling race horses.

But now, all the dazzle of money and society seemed to crumble into emptiness.

It's funny, she thought. Money can't buy happiness. Money couldn't win the war. Money couldn't bring peace. And when you die, money can not buy back one more minute of time.

A rich man's wealth is his strong city, And like a high wall in his own imagination.
(Proverbs 18:11 ASV)

The only thing that was real was her Saviour. Now, more than ever before, the reality of her salvation in Christ became apparent. And she clung to the precious promises she had learned as a child. But her heart ached. Why, oh why, didn't she learn more of these truths then. There it was...the entire blueprint of tomorrow laid out for her in the Bible. And she had squandered her time on charlatans and personal gain. The agony of regret seemed more than she could bear. The events around her were happening too fast. She could not think straight. She was like a little baby...helpless...waiting to be led.

Suddenly, a noise distracted her. Abel came bounding through the door. His face was ashen white.

She had never seen him this way. He looked pitiful. She felt so sorry for him. She wanted to hold him in her arms.

She had never felt like this before. Abel was always the master of his ship. But now it seemed like Abel's ship was without a rudder.

"Sylvia, grab your bags and hurry. We've got to get out of here!"

"Why, honey. Where can we go?"

"This place is a holocaust. Megiddo is one vast burial ground ...dead all over...sickening blood like a miry swamp. You should have seen it. I was lucky to get out alive. Even Dr. Curter is dead! Stop wasting time, Sylvia...let's get moving. There's a Concorde jet at Lod airport. I've given orders to hold the flight till we get there. We're flying to New York!"

"Abel, sit down and let's reappraise the situation. Don't you see there's nothing either of us can do. The King has arrived. Terry told me about it. It's all written in the Book of Revelation and it's actually coming true."

"Sylvia, stop listening to those fairy tales. Besides I don't accept the New Testament."

"I know that Abel, but the same prophecies are written in Daniel, Isaiah, Zechariah and Joel as well. You've witnessed the Battle of Armageddon. Tell me, where is Brother Bartholomew?"

"How did you know he disappeared?"

"I didn't, Abel, but if he did, he was Antichrist, and he's been cast into the Lake of Fire."

"Now I know you're having hallucinations, Sylvia. We've got to get out of here."

"Honey, listen to me...there's no time to lose. Let's get down on our knees now. Ask the Lord Jesus Christ to come into your heart. Accept Him as your Saviour...please darling."

And he shall plant the tabernacles of his palace between the seas in the glorious holy mountain; yet he shall come to his end, and none shall help him.
(Daniel 11:45)

Darling...funny, she had rarely called Abel darling. She slipped her arm about his waist. He seemed like a frightened boy now. For the first time in her life she felt a deep passionate love

For the first time in her life she felt a deep passionate love for him. Abel, the cold, cool, millionaire now needed an understanding love.

for him. Abel, the cold, cool, millionaire now needed an under-standing love. She quietly tried to open the Word of God to him...as much as she could remember...she told him that his Messiah, his Redeemer had come...and soon for those who would not believe, would come an unbelievable and irreversible judgment. For a moment she thought he was on the verge of believing...his eyes moistened. Gently she brushed away a tear. He was about to speak.

A loud explosion outside their window jolted him to reality.

Cursing, he threw her down to the floor.

"Sylvia, you can have your heartless God. I've got my money in New York. And that's where I'm going. I'll buy my way into your Heaven...if there is one!"

The sleek Concorde supersonic airliner...all $35 million of it...was about to start its engines on the Lod airport runway when Abel Epstein rushed up to the gates. He was quickly waved on.

He settled back in the soft, cushioned seats and ordered a cocktail from the stewardess. Abel Epstein had done it again. He'd show this God a lesson or two.

The stewardess came back. "Sorry, sir, we have no liquor anymore. All aircraft have been taken over by other personnel. Would you care for a glass of milk or a soft drink?"

Abel was furious and was about to vent his fury on the helpless stewardess. But he had second thoughts when he looked at her hand.

She was carrying a Bible.

He pushed his seat back into

And again I say unto you, It is easier for a camel to go through the eye of a needle, than for a rich man to enter into the kingdom of God.
(Matthew 19:24)

[God] who hath saved us... not according to our works... but according to His own purpose and grace.
(2 Timothy 1:9)

For by grace are ye saved through faith; and that not of yourselves; it is the gift of God: Not of works, lest any man should boast.
(Ephesians 2:9)

And when Simon saw that through laying on of the apostles' hands the Holy Ghost was given, he offered them money,

Saying, Give me also this power, that on whomsoever I lay hands, he may receive the Holy Ghost.

But Peter said unto him, Thy money perish with thee, because thou hast thought that the gift of God may be purchased with money.
(Acts 8:18-20)

the reclining position and closed his eyes. Soon, he thought, I will be in New York with 10 million other sensible people and things will be back to normal. It was all a bad dream, he comforted himself...a bad dream.

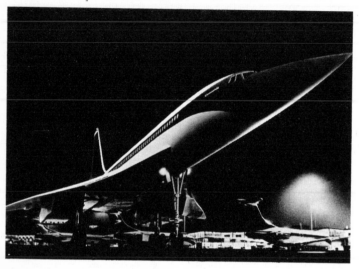

The Concorde Jet took off for the some 6000 mile journey. His face curled into a smile. He would be in New York in about 3 hours! Sylvia could quote all the verses she wanted to...but he wouldn't be there to hear them. She ought to read Proverbs 19:13. That was one verse he often quoted to her: "...a nagging wife annoys like constant dripping."

If Abel Epstein knew that this very moment his financial adviser, George Henderson, was winging his way to Jerusalem he would have lost every sense of security.

His slumber would not be for long. He was to find in New York an unforgettable picture of tragedy and terror.

He could stand no more surprises. But this one would be the biggest!

* * *

Sylvia looked into the mirror. Her hair was a mess. The tears had etched a path down her face. Yet she was no longer concerned about external beauty.

"Abel, dear Abel, why didn't you listen to me. Oh, God, please dear God, save him. I'll do anything for you. Just please save him."

It was some time later she finally found George and Faye with Terry Malone.

Between choking tears she poured out her story to them.

As she looked into their faces, she knew they understood... understood, perhaps too well.

"Sylvia, have you ever heard of Kadesh-Barnea?"

"No, George, why?"

"Well, just before Helen, Bill and Tom left us, they said they were accompanying the Redeemer to Ain Quedeirat."

"What's that?" Sylvia inquired.

"Ain Quedeirat is the Wilderness of Paran, known in Bible days as Kadesh-Barnea. It is in the area called the Arabah which means desert or plain. This is in the Sinai Peninsula. It is a desolate and nearly empty land. It has been the route for many armies. In this area Moses received the Ten Commandments. The Jews wandered here for 40 years.

The Sinai Peninsula itself is 260 miles long and 150 miles wide between the Gulf of Suez and Gulf of Aqaba. If you remember your Bible story, this was the site

And I will bring you into the wilderness of the people, and there will I plead with you face to face.

(Ezekiel 20:35)

of the famous 'Grasshopper Retreat.' It was in Numbers, chapter 13, where God instructed Moses...I forget the rest."

"I know, Dad," Faye chimed in, "God told Moses to take one leader from each tribe and send spies into the land of Canaan. And 40 days later they came back to the wilderness of Paran at Kadesh. Caleb told the group to go up and possess the land... but they said, 'We felt like grasshoppers before them, they were so tall.' I remember Mom telling me that story."

"That's right, Faye, and they all cried to go back to Egypt. And that's when judgment fell."

"What's that have to do with what's happening now?" Sylvia pleadingly inquired.

Mount Nebo, from which Moses viewed the Promised Land.

Just then a messenger ran up to George Omega.

"You're wanted on the phone, sir. You may take it on the phone in the Intercontinental Hotel lobby. It's a transatlantic call, sir."

George picked up the phone. It was his boss at World Television network.

"Get over to Kadesh-Barnea," he screamed. "Some religious fanatics here have told me something's about to happen there."

"When did you get religion, Walter Brinks?"

"I didn't. Don't be stupid...but these characters have been hitting some predictions right on the button...as though they've been reading it in a book...all planned ahead. It's uncanny! And I want a scoop. They tell me the next big event is some kind of a judgment of the nation Israel. And its going to take place in Kadesh-Barnea...some forsaken place in the Sinai Peninsula. Their Redeemer is going to make a personal appearance."

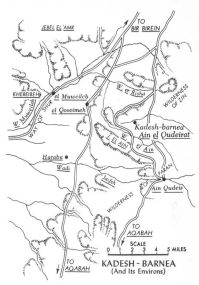

KADESH - BARNEA
(And Its Environs)

"You mean the Messiah, Jesus Christ?"

"Call Him what you want, Omega...but think of the ratings. We'll outpull the old Johnny Carson show. It'll be the scoop of the century. Get a couple mobile TV units there at the King David Hotel and high tail it down to this Kadesh place. As soon as you get there, I want you on the air. We'll telecast via orbiting satellite. I've cleared everything."

George related the entire conversation to Faye, Terry and Sylvia. And much against his will he let them accompany him to Kadesh-Barnea.

Their race against time seemed useless. For when they arrived at Kadesh-Barnea all was still. Occasionally a band of Bedouins with a troop of camels would pass, and one would hear his rhythmic Arabic voice prodding the camels on.

"I wonder if Moses knew then that the sons of his sons would wander here still contending with a Pharaoh?" George mused.

* * *

Whatever was happening, Abel Epstein didn't like it. Suddenly it seemed like an invisible army was rounding up everyone of Jewish extraction...assigning them to ships in the harbor.

Epstein had gathered all his negotiable money and joined the others. Some were singing a song, "How the Oppressor has ceased!" It didn't make sense. Some seemed hilariously happy. Others

...thou shalt take up this proverb against the king of Babylon, and say, How hath the oppressor ceased! The golden city ceased!
(Isaiah 14:4)

like Epstein were confused and sad. Where in the world was this ship going? Who in the world ever heard of this Kadesh place?

It didn't matter. He was tired of running. He fell asleep comforted by a money belt bulging with cash.

Who are these that fly as a cloud, and as the doves to their windows?

Surely the isles shall wait for me, and the ships of many lands first, to bring the sons of Israel home again from far away, their silver and their gold with them, unto the name of the Lord thy God, and to the Holy One of Israel, because He hath glorified thee.

(Isaiah 60:8-9)

* * *

From George Omega's specially built TV booth he had a panorama picture of the action at Kadesh-Barnea. Soon the "ON" light would signal time for his telecast. How he wished he knew more about Bible prophecy. Outside of a few externals he had no idea what was about to happen.

Suddenly from nowhere, it seemed, Helen was by his side.

"But darling, where did you come from and how could you? The doors are closed and we're 50 feet high."

"Honey, you must remember I have been resurrected in Christ. Resurrected believers are not constrained by physical barriers. Besides you'll need help in this telecast."

With that the signal to broadcast lit up.

"This is George Omega reporting to you from Kadesh-Barnea, which is right outside of Israel, to the east. They say nothing is new under the sun. But what we are about to see today will not only be new, but to some, unbelievable. I understand the Redeemer...Christ, the Messiah, will actually be here. This will be His first appearance on television and certainly His first appearance on earth since the resurrection. It will be an historic occasion...yet one edged with much tragedy and also triumph. With me by my side is my wife, Helen."

"Helen is different...that is she was taken up in the Rapture... now she has a new resurrected body. It appears to look just like ours. I recognize her. Yet it is a perfect body, free from the ailments and the aging that still plague us."

"She is living in a new dimension without the restraints of time and space. Yet the marvelous thing about this is that I can communicate with her and she is still, and more so, my attractive Helen."

"You may ask how can I tell a resurrected believer from a living believer? Actually, it's very easy. Helen, as all resurrected believers, has an inner glow of perfection and somehow, don't ask me how, her entire silhouette is edged in a luminous glow."

> It is sown a natural body; it is raised a spiritual body. There is a natural body, and there is a spiritual body.
>
> For our conversation [citizenship] is in heaven: from whence also we look for the Saviour, the Lord Jesus Christ:
>
> Who shall change our vile body, that it may be fashioned like unto His glorious body, according to the working whereby He is able even to subdue all things unto Himself.
>
> (1 Corinthians 15:44)
> (Philippians 3:20-21)

"Helen, I am sure you can fill in the details of this occasion."

Helen, realizing far more the awe of this event, gently touched George's hand in understanding.

"I don't know how to begin," she started, "for what we are about to see here is not pleasant. The Millennium of 1000 years is soon to begin and what we will witness is often called the JUDGMENT OF THE NATION ISRAEL".

"God's chosen people are now back in Israel to stay. Their long years of wandering are over. Their Messiah, and ours, will never again hide His face from His people."

"What we are about to see here is the Judgment of Israel in fulfillment of Ezekiel 20:33-38 which tells us:

> ...it shall come to pass, when all these things are come upon thee, the blessing and the curse, which I have set before thee, and thou shalt call them to mind among all the nations, whither the Lord thy God hath driven thee,
>
> And shalt return unto the Lord thy God, and shalt obey His voice according to all that I command thee this day, thou and thy children, with all thine heart, and with all thy soul;

'...I shall be king over you. And I shall bring you out from the peoples and gather you from the lands where you are scattered...

And I shall bring you into the wilderness of the peoples, and there I shall enter into judgment with you face to face.

As I entered into judgment with your fathers in the wilderness of the land of Egypt, so I will enter into judgment with you...

And I shall make you pass under the rod, and I shall bring you into the bond of the covenant;

And I shall purge from you the rebels and those who transgress against Me...they will not enter the land of Israel. Thus you will know that I am the Lord.'"

Helen turned to continue but Sylvia's tears broke the silence.

"Not my Abel, not my precious Abel...God can't be that cruel!" she sobbed.

Startled, George Omega grabbed the microphone. "I'm sorry for that interruption, and yet God's judgments are sure. Sylvia is one of our best friends, yet her husband failed to accept the Redeemer as King."

Sylvia frustrated and angry dashed to the elevator that quickly whisked her to the ground level.

She could never forget what she saw. All over the plain were what appeared to be millions of people,

That THEN the Lord thy God will turn thy captivity, [restore your fortunes] and have compassion upon thee, and will return and gather thee from all the nations whither the Lord thy God hath scattered thee.

If any of thine be driven out unto the outmost parts of heaven, from thence will the Lord thy God gather thee, and from thence will he fetch thee:

And the Lord thy God will bring thee into the land which thy fathers possessed, and thou shalt possess it; and He will do thee good, and multiply thee above thy fathers.

And the Lord thy God will cleanse thine heart, and the heart of thy seed, to love the Lord thy God with all thine heart, and with all thy soul, that thou mayest live.

(Deuteronomy 30:1-6)

...Thus saith the Lord God; Behold, I will take the children of Israel from among the heathen, whither they be gone, and will gather them on every side, and bring them into their own land:

And I will make them one nation in the land upon the mountains of Israel; and one king shall be king to them all: and they shall be no more two nations, neither shall they be divided into two kingdoms any more at all;

And David my servant shall be king over them; and they all shall have one shepherd: they shall also walk in my judgments, and observe my statutes, and do them.

And they shall dwell in the land that I have given unto Jacob my servant, wherein your

lined in formation according to their final residence. Quickly she ran to the New York line. Almost instantly she spotted Abel.

Breaking through the barriers, it seemed with superhuman effort, she grabbed Abel's arm and pulled him away from the crowd. Hysterically she half carried him to an open place directly in front of the TV cameras.

fathers have dwelt; and they shall dwell therein, even they, and their children, and their children's children for ever: and my servant David shall be their prince for ever.
(Ezekiel 37:21-22,24-25,28)

And I will plant them upon their land, and they shall no more be pulled up out of their land which I have given them, saith the Lord thy God.
(Amos 9:15)

There in splendor beyond words was a Throne. Her eyes so filled with tears, she looked up at the person on the Throne. Though her vision blurred, no one had to tell her. Little Sylvia Epstein was face to face with her Saviour.

She knew what she must do. Tearing the buttons from Abel's shirt she yanked the money belt from around his waist. Abel seemed in a trance, like a little boy, starry eyed and speechless.

She flung the belt at the foot of the Throne.

In an impassioned plea she cried: "Here, Abel, give your all... all your money...I love him, Lord. He doesn't deserve to die. He always gave to the United Jewish Appeal. He even bought Israeli bonds...Look at this money. There must be a million dollars... Abel, give it to the Lord for the rebuilding of Israel...Oh, Abel, repent."

And even as she hysterically spoke she saw no sign of repentance in Abel's stony face. Fear, yes; repentance, no. Her head bowed. It was too late!

Her Redeemer looked down. It was a look of both compassion and of judgment. The voice of what sounded like an angel then came from the side of the throne and thundered across the plains:

> Why should I fear in days of adversity,
> When the iniquity of my foes surrounds me,
> Even those who trust in their wealth,
> And boast in the abundance of their riches
> No man can by any means redeem his brother,

She flung the money belt at the foot of the Throne. In an impassioned plea she cried: "...I love him, Lord. He doesn't deserve to die."

Or give to God a ransom for him —
For the redemption of his soul is costly...
For he sees that even wise men die...
And leave their wealth to others.
This is the way of those who are foolish
As sheep they are appointed for the realm of the dead
And their form shall be for Sheol to consume. [1]

The One upon the throne then waved His arm. George Omega continued the telecast, saying,

"Two men are escorting Abel Epstein to a judgment platform whose ceiling is one that appears to be luminous rod. There are two runways extending out, as one passes through...almost like separating sheep. Epstein is now under the rod...."

"George", Helen added, "if I may interrupt. This is the final fulfillment of the Old Testament Scripture from Malachi 3:2-5. Let me read it to our audience:

'...who can endure the day of His coming? And who can stand when He appears? For He is like a refiner's fire and like fullers' soap (bleaching the dirtiest garments).

He will sit as a...purifier of silver, and He will purify the Levites (the ministers of God). At that time my punishments will be quick and certain.'"

"This is exactly what we are seeing here."

"Yes, Helen, Abel Epstein is now being led away and off of the platform. The swinging door to life and freedom on the right has closed. The only possible route now is the runway to the left. This leads to a transportation column of what appears to be an endless chain of busses. It's hard to describe. Epstein seems meek and unresponsive as though all life has suddenly left him."

"What we have witnessed here is sorrow at Sinai!"

Amid the tears, Faye whispered something into Terry's ear.

Those few words she uttered took but a few seconds, but they were going to have their effect for 1000 years!

---

[1] Psalm 49:5-15

Chapter 3

VALLEY OF TEARS

This was a time when George Omega should be happy but recent events troubled him.

The scene he had witnessed where suddenly some 8 million Jews were separated like sheep and goats...left an indelible impression on him. For from his early days on television there were many among these whom he could recall as his real friends.

They lifted him out of a poverty pocket TV announcing occupation, to one of prominence in New York on a major network.

And George Omega couldn't forget this kindness and concern.

Helen sensed this as he sat rather dejectedly in his Jerusalem apartment overlooking the Valley of Kidron.

George chose this location for his living quarters because he had often stayed here in his search for the identity of Brother Bartholomew. He came to love the site. And on his own he had prepared a TV documentary on the importance of this valley throughout history.

"David's City," as he liked to call Jerusalem, was bounded by two valleys. The valley most visible today is the Valley of Kidron. It lies on the extreme east. On the extreme south and west was the Valley of Hinnom.

Between the Kidron Valley east of the city and the Hinnom Valley on the south and west, there was a smaller central valley. Gradually, through the years, this central valley became filled

The Kidron Valley in Jerusalem.

with debris and its level rose, so that now it seems like an ordinary street in the Old City, leaving no division between ancient eastern and western ridges.

It was here that Christ and His disciples about 30 A.D. crossed the Kidron valley to the Mount of Olives to Gethsemane. But many years before this, David crossed the Kidron in his escape from his rebellious son, Absalom.

> And all the country wept with a loud voice, and all the people passed over: the king himself passed over the brook Kidron, and all the people passed over, toward the way of the wilderness.
> (2 Samuel 15:23)

Through the Kidron valley occasionally there ran a seasonal torrent, the Brook Kidron. This, however, was dry much of the time even in a rainy year. Asa, third king of Judah (964-923 B.C.),

> And also Maachah his mother, even her he removed from being queen, because she had made an idol in a grove; and Asa destroyed her idol, and burnt it by the brook Kidron.
> (1 Kings 15:13)

a godly King deposed his wicked grandmother, a daughter of Absalom, and burned her idol at this Brook Kidron.

And in the old 1967 6-Day War the Israeli Army crossed the ancient Valley of Kidron and ascended the Mount of Olives in their final act of victory.

George spoke, so moved by recent events, as though he was addressing a television audience...although gathered around him were only his loved ones...his wife, Helen, Sue, Tommy, Bill and Faye Sanders, Tom and Terry Malone and Sylvia.

"This is Jerusalem..." He paused to mask the tears in his voice.

"Jerusalem...a recorded history of over 4000 years...perched high amid the Judean hills...the city of David...the city of Solomon's Temple...the city of Isaiah and Jeremiah, giant prophets."

> Nevertheless for David's sake did the Lord his God give him a lamp in Jerusalem, to set up his son after him, and to establish Jerusalem:

"Jerusalem...a city where every stone, ages old or recent, represents a drop in time...."

And then with a twinge of bitterness in his voice, George

> Because David did that which was right in the eyes of the Lord, and turned not aside from any thing that he commended him all the days of his life, save only in the matter of Uriah the Hittite.
> (1 Kings 15:4-5)

continued...

"Jerusalem...is first and foremost a city of war, taken, lost, retaken nearly 50 times within the last 3000 years. Ironic, isn't it, from childhood we've been told to pray for the peace of Jerusalem. What peace? All I've seen here in the last few days is intense sorrow and suffering."

> **Pray for the peace of Jerusalem: they shall prosper that love thee.**
>
> **(Psalm 122:6)**

George still had the scene at Sinai deeply etched in his mind, and what he felt to be the unfairness of it all, was finally beginning to surface.

He continued: "Jerusalem...a city of peace. Why God Himself referred to its habitants as men of Sodom and Gomorrah."

> **Except the Lord of hosts had left unto us a very small remnant, we should have been as Sodom, and we should have been like unto Gomorrah.**
>
> **Hear the word of the Lord, ye rulers of Sodom; give ear unto the law of our God, ye people of Gomorrah.**
>
> **(Isaiah 1:9-10)**

Helen interrupted: "George, Jerusalem is the city of righteousness. In Isaiah 1:21-26 we have a completed picture. We can't just look at the past, but in God's overall design. Let me read it to you:

> How the faithful city has become a harlot,
> She who was full of justice!
> Righteousness once lodged in her...
> Your silver has become dross...
>
> Therefore the Lord God of hosts,
> The Mighty One of Israel declares,
> I will be relieved of My adversaries,
> And avenge Myself on My foes.
>
> I will also turn My hand against you,
> And will smelt away your dross as with lye,
> And will remove all your alloy.
>
> Then I will restore your judges as the first,
> And your counselors as at the beginning;
> After that you will be called the city of righteousness,
> A faithful city."

There were tears now in Helen's eyes as she continued:

"George, don't you see? Our Messiah is a refiner burning off the worthless to prepare us for an eternity of perfect peace and rest. These so-called friends...in your eyes...the eyes of a mere human may appear to be lasting and worthwhile. But God looks at them through the microscope of His perfectness. We may not understand His ways but we know His ways are the best."

> O the depth of the riches both of the wisdom and knowledge of God! How unsearchable are His judgments, and His ways past finding out!
> (Romans 11:33)

"George, if you could see beyond today...into God's eternal tomorrow, and if you could project the actions of your friends in tomorrow's eternity in Heaven then you would know that God's ways are always best."

Tommy, George's son, spoke: "Dad, look at me, your own son. Remember the time I broke my leg in football. Despite all the doctors did one leg was shorter than the other. I walked with a limp. Now look at me. No limp. Perfect. I wore glasses. Now look at me. No glasses. Perfect."

> Surely, you will be ashamed of the oaks which you have desired, And you will be embarrassed at the gardens which you have chosen.
> For you will be like an oak whose leaf fades away, Or as a garden that has no water.
> And the strong man will become tinder, His work also a spark. Thus they shall both burn together, And there will be none to quench them.
> (Isaiah 1:29-31 ASV)

"And Dad," Sue chimed in, "remember when you last saw me. I was just a little child. But now I'm a full grown young woman. Remember at birth when you discovered I only had 3 fingers on each hand. Now look at me, Dad...look at my hands!"

With that she thrust her hands in front of her.

George, startled, looked closely. There were two beautiful hands...complete.

At the moment Helen thought she was getting through, Sylvia suddenly burst into tears.

"It's alright for you to be so happy...like you belong to an exclusive club. But what about me? What about my Abel? Suppose you had seen your husband literally dragged from New York out to that forsaken desert and judged like some criminal?

And without even a chance to say goodbye...hustled off to..." her voice trailed.

The air was tense.

"To where?" Sylvia screamed. "To where, Helen? Tell me WHERE?"

As a living believer, Helen would never have been able to contain herself. Most likely she would have broken down and cried. But now, in her new body as a resurrected believer, perfect in Christ, an inner glow provided peace and understanding.

"Sylvia, we must face reality. Abel rejected His Messiah as Lord, and because he did not accept His Lord's free offer of pardon by accepting Jesus as his Saviour he had to stand in judgment for his sins. He will be cast into the Lake of Fire."

"How can God do this?" Sylvia cried convulsively. "How can a God of love condemn a man like my Abel to an eternity of suffering? Does He have no heart?"

> ...cast...the unprofitable servant into outer darkness: there shall be weeping and gnashing of teeth.
>
> **(Matthew 25:30)**

"That's just it, Sylvia. God is a God of love...He told us in 1 John 2:15,17:

> Do not love the world, nor the things in the world.
> If any man love the world, the love of the Father
> is not in him.
>
> And the world is passing away, and also its lusts;
> but the one who does the will of God abides forever."

"God so loved the world, He gave His own son, Jesus Christ to redeem the world. You remember reading that in John 3:16. And verse 17 tells us that

> ...God did not send the Son into the world to
> judge the world; but that the world should be
> saved through Him."

"How can a God of love condemn someone to Hell?" Helen continued. "God doesn't condemn anyone to an eternity in the Lake of Fire. God provided a way out. If we don't choose to accept His way...we cannot blame God. It was there...the way of escape."

Tom Malone interrupted. "You see, Sylvia, God provided an atonement, a sacrifice since time immemorial. All man had to do was accept it. It's as simple as that."

"But I tried to tell Abel to repent and to give the Messiah all his money. You saw me throw it on the ground," Sylvia reminded him.

For God sent not His Son into the world to condemn the world; but that the world through Him might be saved.

He that believeth on Him is not condemned: but he that believeth not is condemned already, because he hath not believed in the name of the only begotten Son of God.

(John 3:17-18)

Tom continued: "Sylvia in Proverbs 14:12 we were told

There is a way which seems right to a man.

But its end is the way of death."

By this time Sylvia was sobbing hysterically. Sue went over, placed her arms around her shoulders trying to comfort her. But it was to no avail.

Helen felt she must continue: "Sylvia, God provided a way and He is a God of love. But when man chooses not to follow that way and rejects His sacrifice...God then becomes also a God of judgment. It was not a loving God who condemned Abel to hell. It was Abel who condemned himself because he would not accept the atonement provided by God through His son, Christ Jesus. And in Hebrew 2:3 we are told,

"How shall we escape if we neglect so great salvation?"

"I'm sorry, Sylvia, but you just have to face reality."

Sylvia's body shook with sobs.

George looked pale and worried.

Faye gripped Bill's hand. Somehow this whole scene was too much for her emotionally. Was the room too hot? Suddenly everything seemed to be spinning. Bill, Tom and Terry Malone ...everyone just became a sea of faces wrapped in a transparent gauze. Faye got up from her chair in an attempt to get some fresh air.

But her feet were like the wobbly legs of a marionette...and the strings wouldn't move.

Faye collapsed and lay still on the floor!

As George Omega stared at Faye, now resting on the couch, his mind wandered back a few years to Walter Brinks...a man who habitually took cat-naps on his huge office couch. Walter Brinks had been a self-made man. He believed in stepping on people. He often remarked to George Omega, "Georgie, boy... you want to know how to climb the ladder to success? The ladder to success is built on a mass of broken bodies. The more bodies you pile up...the higher up on the ladder you get. Learn to use people...step on them until you get to the top. Then you're king of the realm. That's when you've got power. And no one... I mean NO ONE can take it away from you!"

For a while it appeared that Walter Brinks was right. His theory had quickly landed him a top executive job at World Television Network. He was gruff but somehow George liked him. But whenever he gave George an overseas assignment he hounded him for scoops. In a way, Walter Brinks was fearless, too. George had seen him walk into the center of riots to get an

George remembered those last few years...the long food lines... the impossible taxes...the fight for job openings.

For many days no city in the United States had seen the sun...a pall of grey death hovered over most of the world.

on-the-spot interview...while police and rioters were still exchanging gunfire. Walter even carried his own gas mask. He was not one to let a little tear gas interrupt his news scoops. Often George watched him laugh hilariously as he repeated the story of how all the reporters ran from scenes of disturbances rubbing their eyes...while "little old gas-masked me got right into the center of things."

George remembered those last few years. Each year the riots became more and more intense. They were measured in terms of casualties on both sides...soldiers, police, and civilians. Any little thing touched off a riot...the inability of some to get hospital treatment, the long food lines...the impossible taxes...the fight for job openings.

There were just so many people on earth that jobs became scarce. Schools, as known in the late 1970's, were a thing of the past. Industries had set up specialized learning centers. Young people seemed like men from outer space with computers plugged into their heads. George remembered calling these changes to the attention of Walter Brinks.

"George," Brinks replied, "you're just old fashioned, I'm afraid. This is progress, man...real progress. Think how far we've advanced in the last 30 years. We can control population growth through vaccination. We can control riots by infiltrating water systems of troubled cities with a pacifying drug. We can control human behavior. And one day we will be able to control our environment."

Brinks admitted that controlling the environment still was a problem. For many days no city in the United States had seen the sun. For the last few years a pall of grey death hovered over most of the world. Pollutants had so affected the minds of people that they did things they normally would not do.

"Mentally disturbed by the lead poisoning and oxygen deficiencies in the air—it's no wonder some of our population is acting erratically, George...but times will get better. I can feel it in my bones."

George had not been so sure. And often he had talked to his boss about the events of the Rapture. But each time Brinks would wave him off with a laugh.

"George," he said jokingly, "if God ever comes down and judges us Gentiles, you can bet I'll be the first one on the spot to televise the occasion." And then reflecting on the possibility, he continued, "Think of the commercial time we could sell. We could sell one minute for a quarter of a million dollars. Look at me, George. One day I'll be President of this network."

An office boy interrupted Walter Brinks, waking him from his reflective thought.

"Sir, something unusual's happening in the halls. There's talk of an armada of ships in the harbor...there's...there's...."

"Stop stammering boy...out with it."

"People have suddenly lost their ability to control themselves sir. I saw it with my own eyes. Men and women...looking just like you and I...except they have a luminous type of glow outlining their body...they came in and soon people just started following them...as though they were directed by some unseen force."

"What did they say?" Brinks demanded.

"I heard one of them say the ships were headed for the Middle East and that a judgment of Gentiles was to take place...whatever that means...in some old Bible-type name they called the Valley of Jehos...something."

Walter Brinks made it his business to know everything... including the Bible...although he didn't believe in it.

Almost with devilish joy he shouted, "Valley of Jehoshaphat! What a story! Old George must have been right after all. Judgment of the Gentiles. Now I remember it. Quick, get my limousine. I'm headed for Kennedy International Airport!"

"And on your way out, tell my secretary to get me George Omega in Jerusalem. Use our orbiting satellite phone system. It's quicker."

In a few minutes, George was on the phone:

"George, I've got good news for you. Looks like we're going to have to drop those soap operas for a few days. Big things are happening. Your Judgment of Gentiles is coming up. What a show that will be. But boy will those housewives howl when they see we've taken General Hospital off the air. I'm lining up advertisers for this Special. We'll shoot it from every angle. George, I want you to give me background copy coverage. Sweep the dust off that Bible, George and fill in the details. I want plenty of interviews. And get some of those who are sentenced to death on the tube. Wow...what a scoop! What a day ...what a day. Move...George...move. Remember...George... first those condemned to death...then interview anyone else you want. Money's no object. Offer a cool million to start for exclusive TV rights. That will impress them."

George was dejected. First, Sylvia's outburst, then his own misgivings about the coming Millennium...and now all Walter Brinks could think about was a scoop.

> ...Why doth this generation seek after a sign?...
>
> Having eyes, see ye not? and having ears, hear ye not? and do ye not remember?
>
> (Mark 8:12,18)

He had not yet gotten over the heartsick scene at Kadesh-Barnea where millions of Jews were divided in the judgment of the nation Israel.

Now would he be forced to witness another judgment...that of the Gentiles. Physically he felt he could not hold up...but Brinks had a forceful way about him. One didn't say "No" to Walter Brinks.

From his Mount of Olives apartment George was just a stone's throw away from his television control center.

Just a few days before great changes had occurred in this area. Christ, the Redeemer King had burst through the sky with His army. Helen, Sue, Tommy and Bill Sanders and Tom Malone were in this army. It was a happy occasion...yet tragic.

As the King's feet touched the Mount of Olives...the entire mountain split apart...right in the middle from east to west. It created a huge valley.

George recalled televising this story after it occurred. Brinks was proud of this scoop. He used a split screen. And as George

> And His feet shall stand in that day upon the Mount of Olives, which lies before Jerusalem on the east, and the Mount of Olives shall be split in two from the east to the west by a very great valley; and half of the mountain shall remove toward the north, and half of it toward the south.
>
> (Zechariah 14:4 Amplified Bible)

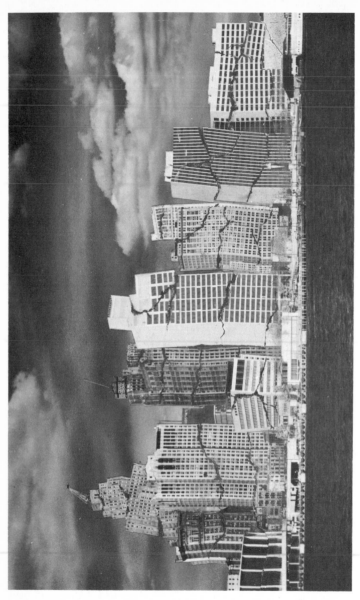

Walter Brinks had the TV cameras pan across the New York skyline even as the earthquake was occurring.

recounted the events and showed how half of the Mount of Olives was to the North and the other half to the South...Brinks showed the destruction of New York City with the flashes of lightening...the booming thunder and the hailstones that weighed nearly 100 pounds.

It was almost with a sense of pride and accomplishment that he had the cameras pan across the New York skyline to show how the earthquake had split the city into three parts.

It seemed like ages ago...although it had only been a few days ago. George was overwhelmed at the sudden speed of events...as though he were flying in a jet plane, 1000 miles per hour ...covering so much territory in so short a time...he just could not fathom its significance. The poles of time were whizzing by so fast ...it all became a blur.

Helen sensed this, motioned to George, and then she began the description of the events.

And there were voices, and thunders, and lightnings; and there was a great earthquake, such as was not since men were upon the earth, so mighty an earthquake, and so great.

And the great city was divided into three parts, and the cities of the nations fell: and great Babylon came in remembrance before God, to give unto her the cup of the wine of the fierceness of His wrath...

And there fell upon men a great hail out of heaven, every stone about the weight of a talent [nearly 100 pounds]: and men blasphemed God because of the plague of the hail; for the plague thereof was exceeding great.
(Revelation 16:18-19, 21)

"George Omega and I are situated at a crest overlooking the Valley of Jehoshaphat. Up till this time it has been known as the Valley of Kidron. But our King and Redeemer has given it a new name...the Valley of Jehoshaphat."

"And quite a significant name it is. For Jehoshaphat means, 'Jehovah judges.' And we are about to witness just that. Jesus Christ, the Redeemer will become Jesus Christ, the Judge."

"From here one can see Jerusalem's East Gate, the Golden Gate, closed for hundreds of years...but now open. This scene

Then said the Lord unto me; This gate shall be shut, it shall not be opened, and no man shall enter in by it; because the Lord, the God of Israel, hath entered in by it, therefore it shall be shut.

It is for the prince; the prince, he shall sit in it to eat bread before the Lord; he shall enter by the way of the porch of that gate, and shall go out by the way of the same.
(Ezekiel 44:2-3)

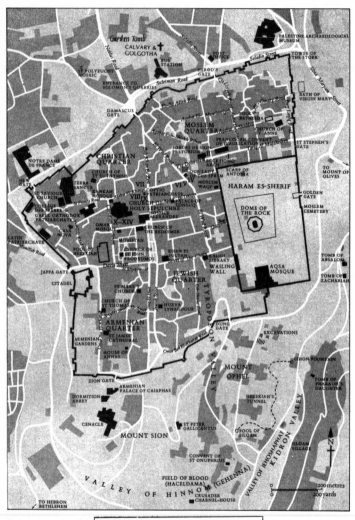

THE OLD CITY OF
JERUSALEM
in the 1970's

looks so impressive from below, from the Valley of Jehoshaphat... but that open gate will serve as a picture of regret for those who failed to claim the promise of redemption. To the right, and far below in the valley is the village of Silwan. This you may recall was the Bible city of Siloam."

"Directly in front of us are several great tombs...the most noticeable is the tomb of Absalom, David's third son. David, incidentally, is soon to become Regent of Jerusalem. You may recall that Absalom was a most handsome man. Once a year he would get a haircut. His cut hair weighed all of 3 pounds."

> **But in all Israel there was none to be so much praised as Absalom for his beauty: from the sole of his foot even to the crown of his head there was no blemish in him.**
>
> **And when he cut the hair of his head he weighed it (for at each year's end he cut it, because its weight was a burden to him) and it weighed 200 shekels by the king's weight.**
> **(2 Samuel 14:25-26**
> **Amplified Bible)**

> **Then said Joab, I may not tarry thus with thee. And he took three spears in his hand, and thrust them through the heart of Absalom, while he was yet alive in the midst of the oak.**
> **(2 Samuel 18:14)**

"Absalom had great designs on King David's throne and, in fact, proclaimed himself King. His selfish greed ended in his own death when his hair became caught in the branches of an oak tree, and his murderers caught him."

"In that last battle, 20,000 men died."

George interrupted. "The Mount of Olives is no longer what it once was, as it appeared in previous centuries, a lonely place where one would wander

> **And the people of Israel were defeated there before the servants of David, and the slaughter there that day was great, 20,000 men.**
>
> **(2 Samuel 18:7)**

and meditate. Today, if one were to name it after the objects most conspicuous on its slopes, it should be called the Mount of Hotels.

"Below us is a scene I find most difficult to describe...a huge sea of a mass of faces...an open area where the Judge sits upon a throne...made from materials I fail to recognize. A luminous glow permeates the spot. I don't know what to say. I just don't..."

Tom Malone stepped in to fill the gap. "George Omega is a young Christian, a Living Believer. Perhaps, I, a Resurrected Believer, can give a more complete account of what you are witnessing on your television screens."

"This is the Judgment of the Gentiles. As Scriptures indicate, it is taking place immediately after the Judgment of the Nation Israel. What we will see are Living Gentiles...not Resurrected Gentiles...who will be judged on the basis of whether they have or have not accepted Christ as Saviour and King. The die has already been cast. It is now too late to change their decision. For those eventually destined to the Lake of Fire...this is a regret they will take with them throughout all of eternity."

"This is a judgment of individuals...not of nations as a whole. Rulers will be judged on the basis of wrongs committed. And their subjects will be judged on whether they obeyed and followed God or men."

Then Peter and the other apostles answered and said, We ought to obey God rather than men.

(Acts 5:29)

"May I repeat, this is a judgment of the Living Gentiles...not the dead. The Great White Throne Judgment will not take place until *after* the 1000 year Millennium. At that time godless leaders, who are presently dead, such as Chairman Mao, Adolph Hitler, Alexei Kosygin and others, will be resurrected and face the final judgment. This is found in Revelation, chapter 20, verses 12 and 15."

"Now, let's go down to the Valley floor to give you a first hand account. George Omega should be there by now. Come in, George."

"This is George Omega...the press of the crowds is unbelievable. The wailing and crying are hard to imagine. If I could rename this place I believe I would call it the Valley of Regret. For here, shortly, for these all of future life will be determined within a few seconds...what many termed a Bible fantasy is suddenly becoming a horrifying reality. Just a moment...the judgment is about to begin."

"A young woman stands before the Redeemer King. She wants to speak and yet words just don't come out. It's like waiting a lifetime to say a poignant speech and then when that moment arrives...one becomes speechless. She fails to look up. Her head is bowed...as though in prayer. Her hand clutches a well-worn Bible. The Redeemer King is about to speak. Let's listen."

> Come, you who are blessed of My Father,
> inherit the kingdom prepared for you
> from the foundation of the world.

"May I step in a moment, George?" Tom Malone inquired. "This is a familiar verse of Scripture taken right from the New Testament book of Matthew, chapter 25, verse 34."

"Thank you, Tom for that background information. And now another steps forth. I can't believe it. It's my own boss. Why it's Walter Brinks. Walter! Walter! What are you doing here?"

"I don't understand it. There is no response. His eyes stare blankly in space as though some unseen power has suddenly made him powerless. He walks toward the Redeemer King but the face has suddenly changed. It's uncanny. It's not a face of kind redemption...but suddenly it appears as the face of a stern judge. He's speaking. He's speaking. I've never seen such an abrupt change of personality.

> Depart from Me, accursed one, into the eternal
> fire which has been prepared for the devil and
> his angels."[1]

George felt weak and horrified.

"Oh no! Oh, this can't be. They can't. He's my boss. My best friend! Where are they taking him?"

...these will go away into eternal punishment[2]

"What about that girl? Is she going there, too?"

...but the righteous into eternal life.[3]

The events and the horror of the day were too much for George Omega. He could not watch anymore. It was all over.

What he longed for...1000 years of happiness...so far had been days of disaster and heart-rending tragedy.

He met Faye and Bill and Helen back at the apartment.

---

[1] Matthew 25:41 [2] Matthew 25:46 [3] Matthew 25:46

Faye was crying as Bill put his arms around her.

That action of love triggered a violent outburst.

"Get away from me, Bill. Look at you...holier than thou... I'm going to have your baby in 7 months...but you're no longer my husband. You're a Resurrected Believer," she said, with a lifting sneer to the tone of her voice.

"And what am I?...a peon on earth. I can look at you. I can even touch you. But I can't love you! I can't love you! Am I going to bring a child in a world like this. All Daddy and I have seen these past few days are terrible judgments. The crying and screaming are driving me crazy. Is that all this new age knows is judgments! Where's the love?"

"A baby!" Bill shouted. "Honey, I'm so happy!"

But George Omega, both surprised at the announcement and shocked, had other thoughts.

Somehow he felt that a worse thing was yet to come.

Little did those in that room realize how true that would be!

Chapter 4

JOURNEY TO JERUSALEM

With Walter Brinks gone, George Omega was quickly summoned to New York. Terry Malone and Sylvia Epstein accompanied him.

He dreaded the flight...because he wanted to remain in Jerusalem where all the action was occurring.

But World Television Network was in a state of chaos. And an urgent transatlantic call made it mandatory that he return to headquarters.

How would the place look, he wondered. All the familiar faces he once knew...would they be gone...would some still be there? Harry Sutherland, one of the vice-presidents at the Network had briefed him via phone...but the conversation was not long.

Harry Sutherland...funny...George thought...never dreamed he was a Christian. He was so quiet...never talked to me about the Bible.

Guess I'll be in for a few surprises, George thought, as the Concorde jet crossed the continent of Europe.

Soon the seat belt sign was turned on and George knew that the answers to many of his questions would be forthcoming shortly.

The pilot was on the intercom.

"Good evening, ladies and gentlemen. Or should I say, good day. We are experiencing some unusual occurrences. In our normal flight schedule this would be evening since we will be landing in New York at 7:30 PM. We are presently 500 miles out at sea and already in our landing pattern. But as you can see, it is not evening. For the past few days a rather surprising phenomena has faced us. We seem to have a perpetual day. Even the moon is reflecting much more light."

"Scientists and agriculturists have told us if such a condition continues it will revolutionize the farm belts throughout the world resulting in increased productivity."

> Moreover the light of the moon shall be as the light of the sun, and the light of the sun shall be sevenfold, as the light of seven days, in the day that the Lord bindeth up the breach of His people, and healeth the stroke of their wound.
>
> (Isaiah 30:26)

Sylvia, who had majored in Ecology in college, also worked for the United States government in Environmental Protection.

"George," she said, "do you realize what is happening? With increased productivity and land reclamation...famine will be abolished. Everyone will have enough to eat. Why even wars could cease. Last year alone 15 million people died of hunger. Apparently the blessings of the Millennium are already starting."

"Sylvia, if that's true," Terry interrupted, "if the Millennium is really starting, won't that mean that there will be other changes taking place on the earth, too? What about the smog and air pollution that has been choking New York City where all private autos were banned last year...where oxygen units were placed in telephone booths throughout the city? Will this change?"

Just then the pilot continued on the intercom: "A bulletin has just been received. I am sure many of you are aware of the tremendous pollution problems we have been faced with not only in America but also throughout the world. Within a radius of 35 miles of Los Angeles alone there are 45 incorporated cities. Within a 60-mile radius of downtown Los Angeles live 12.6 million persons who, up until the recent auto ban, drove 6.9 million cars. Los Angeles was known as the most motorized cluster of human beings in the world. And New York City was not far behind. One in 4 deaths in New York are linked to pollution. This pall of death was reaching frightening proportions because our 7-mile umbrella ceiling that envelopes our entire earth was trapping us. Pollutants, rising in the air, hit this barrier and then came right back down."

"Our whole earth system has become so clogged we were rapidly coming to a standstill. Recent weather reports have indicated some amazing changes. We have just received these announcements. Normally our landing into Kennedy International has to be made solely on instruments, even in daylight ...visibility being less than 1 mile."

"Meteorologists tell us violent updrafts of air in the past few days have apparently created a new atmosphere...like someone opening the door of a smoke-filled room and a draft of air suddenly filling the room expelling the polluted climate. They report it was like lifting the lid off of a pressurized container. Upon release there was a 'whoosh,' and the earth looked like a new baby...no more wrinkled skin of aging."

"What that all comes down to is this...from what can be gathered there is no more 7 mile ceiling enveloping the earth system. All the pollutants in the air have been released into outer space. The air system is bright and clear. All systems are go. Our landing will be a visual approach...and even at 7:30 PM...in BRIGHT DAYLIGHT. What else can I say but PRAISE GOD!"

Everyone on the plane clapped and cheered.

"Unbelievable," George shouted. "Simply unbelievable!"

"Sylvia," Terry exclaimed, "Normally on happy occasions... or when a plane is delayed in takeoff...the pilot orders a round of free drinks for everyone...but now, it's like living a clean life...free of sin. Everyone is so happy...no need for bars or for smoking sections. I've got to pinch myself. I can't believe it's true."

Terry was going to say more but a sudden feeling of faintness caused her to grip her seat and recline to retain her composure.

In every disaster...the looters were there first.

They were even robbing the dead.

The scene at the New York office of World Television Network was hectic. It was like picking up the pieces after a disaster. One of George's first jobs was finding out who was left. Harry Sutherland asked him to call a meeting of all personnel. World Television had employed 1400 people. It was going to be a difficult task. Phone lines were down, rubble filled the streets... many buildings were no longer standing.

"What in the world has happened, Harry?" George exclaimed.

"We've had a severe earthquake here...a few days ago. Many thousands were killed. Who knows, perhaps a million. Fortunately we foresaw the crowded conditions of Manhattan and built ourselves a new, low, one-story headquarters outside the city. Our old building is nothing but a pile of rock. Just a few cracks in the wall here, however. Not serious."

"How did you maintain any order and get things moving again?"

"At first, it seemed impossible. Amazing, in the midst of crisis... the New York labor unions were fighting as to who would remove the rubble, squabbles and strikes erupted over 'hazardous and over-time pay.' Undertakers were demanding cash in advance for funerals and grave diggers were picketing funeral parlors because many of the bodies were buried in a common grave...thus cutting out a major part of their income."

And there were voices, and thunders, and lightnings; and there was a great earthquake, such as was not since men were upon the earth, so mighty an earthquake, and so great.

And the great city was divided into three parts, and the cities of the nations fell: the great Babylon came in remembrance before God, to give unto her the cup of the wine of the fierceness of his wrath.

(Revelation 16:18-19)

"I can't believe it, Harry!"

"There was much more. The looting was unbelievable. Where all the people came from I don't know...but they drove in like hordes from as far away as Akron, Ohio and Greenville, North Carolina. Some even came down from Canada. Before rescuers could begin their work...the looters were there robbing the dead. In fact...do you remember the Canadian seal episode where seals were clubbed to death and then skinned?"

"Yes, I recall."

"Remember, that many seals did not die from the blows... but were simply stunned. And money-hungry hunters skinned them alive. What I saw a few days ago, I could never believe. I still get nauseated thinking of it. And I know it's true because I witnessed it myself. Some people were lying under a pile of rubble. What I thought were rescuers were feverishly lifting the rocks. This was on Wall Street. When they reached the bodies which appeared dead...they methodically went through their pockets pulling out their wallets, ripping off their wrist watches. A few started to move. I ran over to stop them...but one burly fellow pinned my arms back while his friends did the dirty work. And this, you will not believe. One man they called 'pliers Joe' pulled a pair of pliers from his pocket...they looked like a dental tool. He yanked open this one man's mouth, secured the plier to a gold tooth and pulled."

"George, the man was not dead, the earthquake had simply stunned him...and the pulling of his tooth brought him to his senses screaming hysterically...and trying to get up. Before I could do anything 'pliers Joe' grabbed a hammer from his pocket and brought it crashing down on the poor man's skull. They stripped him of every last cent he had...and went on to the next pile of bodies."

"Harry, I find that hard to believe. Can man actually be that cruel to his fellow man?"

"Such inhumanity is not hard to believe, George. It's been going on for many years. Don't you remember way back in December, 1972, as an example, when that Eastern Air Lines jet crashed in the Everglades? Over 90 were killed. Who were the first people on the scene in the muck and in that eerie darkness? The LOOTERS. And rescue teams said they were methodically robbing the dead...taking watches and wallets. Remember the rescue team report, '...what can you do? We were trying to help the survivors and get them out of there.'"

"I do recall that, Harry. In fact, one Coast Guardsman, a personal friend of mine told me, 'I don't know how people like that get here so fast."

"But tell me, Harry, with all these difficulties...strikes, crime, etc., how has so much order and restoration been achieved?"

"That's what got me digging into Isaiah, Zechariah and Revelation. I was never much of a Christian...as far as witnessing to others. That's why you may have been surprised to see me left. When the earthquake struck, I knew something was happening...went straight to the Bible. Odd, isn't it...for years it gathered dust on my shelf...a good thing to have around for weddings and funerals...a status symbol. Then suddenly, I would have fought off ten men to get hold of a Bible. What was an object of little importance, overnight became my most treasured possession. As I studied hour after hour...I knew that what had occurred was the Battle of Armageddon and soon the Millennium would be ushered in. That meant judgments, first for the Jew and the nation Israel and then for the Gentile."

"I reasoned to myself, if the Bible hit Armageddon on the button for accuracy...then everything else would also fall into place *exactly* as Scriptures said it would. And it has! Shortly after this chaos here, what appeared like an army of men arrived both on ships and space ships!"

"You mean they used our space shuttles, Harry?"

"Yes, just about every means of transportation. You know our advanced delta-winged space shuttles reach an altitude of 25 miles and a speed of 2800 miles per hour *less than two minutes after lift-off.*"

"Who were these men?"

"I later found out they were Resurrected Believers...in fact I recognized some...they worked in our office...died in the early 1970's. Bodies looked like ours...but all physical defects were gone...they never seemed to tire...like superhuman... angel-like. Their silhouette was outlined in a luminous glow. That's the way you could spot them. Walls, ordinary hazards of traffic didn't affect them. And through some unseen power, of God, I am sure, they were able to corral first all living Jews ...and a few days later all Gentiles. I know you couldn't see me in that sea of faces in the Valley of Jehoshaphat but I was there ...and then just as quickly, shuttled back.

"It's like a new world. No more confusion. All of the trouble-makers are now gone. Everyone is working day and (I was almost going to say night)...no more bickering and in a few days we will be back to normal."

"But I've talked enough, George, I understand there is going to be a big meeting in Jerusalem and after you get things in order here, I'd like you to go back to cover it."

"Sir," a secretary interrupted, "telephone for Mr. Omega."

"Excuse me, Harry, I'll take it in my office."

An old familiar chorus crossed George's mind, and he started singing it as he walked to his office...

> One thousand years with Christ the Son;
> One thousand years and they've just begun;
> One thousand years, what wedded bliss!
> One thousand years, what joy is this!

"Hello, this is George Omega."

"George, come over to the apartment, quick. It's Terry, she's sick, dreadfully sick!"

"What's wrong, Sylvia? She seemed alright on the plane."

"Can't talk now, George. Please hurry."

* * *

Terry looked like a little child tucked in among the clean white hospital covers. Her pale face seemed to blend in with the pillow. Her long silken blonde hair was disheveled. There was no doubt about it. Terry was a sick girl.

George had no time to ask questions when he arrived at the apartment. Foremost in his mind was rushing her to the hospital.

"Terry," he said, "I've been so busy, I haven't had a chance to call Tom. I'll call him now."

Suddenly Terry's eyes opened. "No, oh, no, please George, please don't call Tom now. You'll only worry him...and me. Please, George."

"But Terry, you're sick...Terry, what do you feel is wrong with you?"

"Nothing, George, nothing, it's probably something I ate on the plane. Suddenly I felt woozy and weak."

Dr. Leyton walked in with his nurse.

"Mr. Omega, would you mind sitting in the waiting room a few minutes while we give Mrs. Malone an initial examination. It won't take long. I'll be out shortly to inform you of my findings."

A thousand and one things raced into George's mind as he sat in the waiting room. There was so much to do...another flight back to Jerusalem...and now Terry added to the complications. George had left Sylvia at the house, much to her reluctance, requesting she pack for their flight back to Jerusalem.

Just then Sylvia popped in.

"Sylvia, what on earth are you doing here? Why aren't you packing?"

"George, I'm the fastest packer this side of Madison Avenue. I'm worried about Terry. She isn't her usual self. You know, I think she's..."

Dr. Leyton interrupted the conversation.

"Mr. Omega, where is Mrs. Malone's husband?"

"He's in Jerusalem, Doctor. He is a Resurrected Believer, of course."

"Oh, that may complicate things. When did Mr. Malone die?"

"A little over two months ago, sir. Don't you remember? He was the first to die by guillotine right on a church lawn by Brother Bartholomew."

"A little over two months ago? I'm glad to hear that. I am sure Mr. Malone will be very happy."

"Why, Doctor?"

"Well, he is going to become a father. Terry Malone is pregnant...in her third month."

"I don't believe it," Sylvia stammered joyously. "I don't believe it. Tom will be thrilled. Wow. Think of it, George...first Faye is having a baby and now Terry. That's a double blessing!"

"Let's hope so, Sylvia. Let's pray that both Faye and Terry go full term."

"Mr. Omega...you're a newspaperman but apparently not up on your news. That shouldn't be any problem now...that is, Terry going full term. She's had some initial difficulty that normally would require two weeks of complete bed rest. But in this new Millennial Age our medical techniques have been completely revolutionized."

"In the past, in spite of all man's progress in the science of medicine and surgery, we were still living in a world of suffering and death. Rides past endless miles of homes, hospitals and sanitariums made us aware of this fact."

"Our accident ward and emergency room are just about going out of business. Disease and illness as we know it is already slowing down, we believe, soon to minimal."

And the inhabitant shall not say, I am sick....
(Isaiah 33:24)

No longer will there be in it an infant who lives but a few days, Or an old man who does not live out his days; For the youth will die at the age of one hundred And the one who does not reach the age of one hundred Shall be thought accursed.
(Isaiah 65:20 ASV)

"Never before have I seen so many crutches brought back to this hospital in spite of the recent earthquake devastation we have witnessed. My own nephew who has been deaf and dumb since birth can now hear and speak."

"You will recall in the 60's through the 1980's we relied heavily on antibiotics and chemical derivatives for healing. But in the last few days our swing back

Then the eyes of the blind shall be opened, and the ears of the deaf shall be unstopped.

Then the lame man leap as an hart, and the tongue of the dumb sing: for in the wilderness shall

Think of it, LEAVES, both in crushed and whole form, are providing amazing and quick healing!

to the simple things and our lack of these drugs...has forced us to turn back to herbs...old fashion remedies. In the past they had some limited success. But now we are finding such ordinary things as leaves...think of it, LEAVES, both in crushed and whole form, are providing amazing and quick healing. There is actually power in a simple leaf! God's power!"

> waters break out, and streams in the desert.
> **(Isaiah 35:5-6)**

"That's what we have prescribed for Mrs. Malone. By the morning she'll be as good as new and can accompany you to Jerusalem."

It was a wonderful reunion at Lod airport in Jerusalem. Tom had not been told of the problems that occurred in New York

> And by the river on its bank, on one side and on the other, will grow all kinds of trees for food. Their leaves will not wither, and their fruit will not fail. They will bear every month because their water flows from the sanctuary, and their fruit will be for food and their leaves for healing.
> **(Ezekiel 47:12 ASV)**

nor that Terry was going to have a baby. George, after much thought, felt it better that Terry break the news in her own way upon their return.

What was this new world going to be like? George asked himself. For years he had been dealing with Brother Bartholomew. He knew what that world of tribulation was like. Bartholomew's ruling with an iron fist, crushing those who failed to toe the line.

1000 years...the Millennium...somewhere along the line he was told the Millennial Kingdom would be a *theocracy*. He should know the full impact of that word...theocracy...he mused. Exactly what does that mean?

He pulled a book from his bookshelf...the dictionary. Let me see, R, S, T...Ta...Te...Th...here it is, THEOCRACY. Slowly, he read:

THEOCRACY
1. a form of government in which God or a deity is recognized as the supreme civil ruler.
2. a system of government by priests claiming a divine commission.
3. a state under such a form of government.

George wanted to investigate further. He glanced through THINGS TO COME by J. Dwight Pentecost and quite by accident came to page 502. There was a Scripture reference to the theocratic kingdom in the Millennium. It was found in Isaiah 40:10,

> Behold the Lord God will come with might,
> With His arm ruling for Him...

He checked other translations. What did that mean? "...His arm ruling for Him...?

And there he found it...

> He will rule with awesome strength.

All of his pent-up joy suddenly burst like a balloon. George Omega sunk dejectedly in his chair.

Helen came in to remind him of his appointment in the Temple Court to meet David, Regent of Palestine.

"Why are you troubled, George?"

"Helen, do you realize this Millennial government is a theocracy?"

"Of course I do."

"Do you know what a theocracy is...God will rule with a rod of iron. Is that any different than the seven tortuous years I've been through with Brother Bartholomew? Helen, I don't know...I'm beginning to have my doubts."

"Honey, it's only natural for you to have this reaction. But a theocracy isn't new. A true theocracy was established at the time of creation. God was recognized as sovereign. Part of this sovereignty that belonged to God was delegated to man, who was to rule over the earth in a form of intermediary authority. In that theocracy Adam derived his authority from God."

> Thou shalt break them with a rod of iron; thou shalt dash them in pieces like a potter's vessel.
>
> Be wise now therefore, O ye kings: be instructed, ye judges of the earth.
>
> Serve the Lord with fear, and rejoice with trembling.
>
> Kiss the Son, lest he be angry and ye perish from the way, when His wrath is kindled but a little. Blessed are all they that put their trust in Him.
>
> (Psalm 2:9-12)

"Why can't it be a Republic, where legislative, executive and judicial power is lodged in the people? This would be more democratic? Surely God in this Millennial Age will be a God of love and of grace. With all the unsaved gone...why can't a democratic form of government work perfectly?"

"George, it's true those who have not accepted Christ as Saviour have already been sent to Hades. And at the end of the 1000 years they will go to the Lake of Fire. But you must remember that there are still millions of Living Believers here on earth. Some are married. Other Living Believers will marry. Their conjugal relationships will still enable them to have children...even though such relationships cannot occur with Resurrected Believers. From this union will come children. Earth's population is going to soar."

"Will these babies automatically be Christians without sin?" George asked Helen.

"That's just it, honey," she replied, "you must keep in mind that all those who will be born of Living Believers during this 1000 year Millennial Age will have a sin nature. It will be necessary for them to accept Christ as Saviour and Lord if they are to participate in the final and continuing eternity that begins after the Millennium."

> ...out of them shall proceed thanksgiving and the voice of them that make merry: and I will multiply them, and they shall not be few; I will also glorify them, and they shall not be small.
>
> Their children also shall be as aforetime, and their congregation shall be established before me, and I will punish all that oppress them.
>
> (Jeremiah 30:19-20)

"But what's that all have to do with a Theocracy and a Republic?"

"Our ways are not God's ways. If a theocracy did not exist, positions of leadership could go to unredeemed men and women. God has already given human rule its chance, and it failed miserably. This no doubt is one reason God through Christ will

> Incline your ear, and come unto me: hear, and your soul shall live; and I will make an everlasting covenant with you, even the sure mercies of David.
>
> Behold, I have given him for a witness to the people, a leader and commander to the people.
>
> (Isaiah 55:3-4)

rule with awesome strength. This is one reason why David is Regent of all of Palestine."

"Remember all the talk about a one world system many years ago. It would never work under the government of sinful men. Now we will see a true world government...a unified government...ruled and governed by our King Redeemer. And Israel will no longer be divided."

And I will make them one nation in the land upon the mountains of Israel; and one king shall be king to them all: and they shall be no more two nations, neither shall they be divided into two kingdoms any more at all...

And the heathen shall know that I the Lord do sanctify Israel when my sanctuary shall be in the midst of them for evermore.
(Ezekiel 37:22,28)

Tom Malone kissed the tears from Terry's cheeks.

"Terry, this should be the happiest day of your life. We're going to have a baby. Won't it be something if you and Faye have your baby on the same day."

"It could happen, honey," Terry sobbed.

"Suppose Faye has a boy and we have a girl...and one day they get married. Wouldn't it be a wonderful plan? Bill and I...even though we are Resurrected Believers...will through our children be able to complete a union of love. Honey, don't cry. George told me all about it. You won't lose the baby. Everything will work out great...you'll see."

"Everything will work out great." Those words seemed to unbalance Terry into uncontrollable sobs.

Tom gently placed her on the couch, and tucked her under a blanket. He then kissed her tear stained cheeks.

"I know you're tired honey. The strain's been too much for you. Sylvia will stay with you while you get some much needed rest."

Terry dropped off to sleep with the words, "Everything will work out great" ringing in her ears. Softly she prayed, "I hope so, I hope so."

Chapter 5

LIFE IN THE LEAF

To George Omega, everyday brought a new surprise. George discovered that his new boss at World Television Network was a Living Believer. If anything, he would have believed that Harry's wife, Carole, would have been. In all the rushing of the past few days he forgot to ask about Carole. Carole was on a 21-day Holy Land tour just before everything broke loose.

Come to think of it, he did recall Harry trying to track her down a couple days ago.

In a few minutes George would be on worldwide satellite TV beaming his Special Event newscast back to the United States. So much had changed in the alignment of the nations and in the topography of the world that he knew he would need help. That's why he asked Bill Sanders and Tom Malone along. As Resurrected Believers they would have a thorough grasp of the situation.

Walking to the Temple area he automatically looked for the familiar Dome of the Rock and the more recently built Temple around it, which had been Brother Bartholomew's masterpiece. This eight-sided building, surmounted by a beautifully proportioned dome covered with shiny gold-toned aluminum, had been a sight to behold. He remembered the eight arcades, known as scales or balances, where Moslems believed on Judgment Day a giant set of these balances would be here to weigh the merits of each one.

But the Dome of the Rock and Brother Bartholomew's newer Temple were both gone. An earthquake at the time of the Battle of Armageddon had disintegrated them both.

The Temple area was now a vast court. Construction had already begun on the building of a most elaborate Temple. Construction methods had improved so greatly in the past 30 years that it was anticipated this Temple would be completed within a few short months.

What would it be like to meet David? he mused. Would he be like one of us?

> Then he brought me to the nave and measured the side pillars; six cubits wide on each side was the width of the side pillar...
>
> And He said to me, "Son of man, this is the place of My throne and the place of the soles of My feet, where I will dwell among the sons of Israel forever. And the house of Israel will not again defile My holy name, neither they nor their kings, by their harlotry and by the corpses of their king when they die...
>
> This is the law of the house: its entire area on the top of the mountain all around shall be most holy. Behold, this is the law of the house.
> **(Ezekiel 41:1; 43:7,12 ASV)**

Quickly George, Bill and Tom mounted the stairs leading to the TV telecasting tower.

No sooner had they seated themselves when George's phone rang.

An agitated voice could be heard on the other end.

"George, this is Harry Sutherland. You'll be going on in two minutes. But I need your help. I can't locate Carole. I guess you knew that we hadn't been too close lately. That was one of the reasons I sent her on that Holy Land tour...thought she could get closer to what it's all about. But my personal life hasn't been without fault, either. In all our married life, not once did I talk to her about her need of God. Once I started to but she hit me where it hurts when she replied, 'Don't tell me about your God with all the running around you do!' But I need her now...more than ever before. I've tried every available avenue... I can't even reach the tour guide in East Jerusalem. He was headquartered in the St. George Hotel. George, I'm desperate. She has to be somewhere. I'm going out of my mind!"

"I'll get busy on it right away, Harry...but my ready light is on now. Be in touch, soon."

George turned to face the TV camera and he began his commentary.

"Hello, this is George Omega, once more coming from the heart of Jerusalem. Jerusalem where for years Israel has asked *'Ma ihieh hassof?'* What will be the end? Jerusalem, with a recorded history of some 4000 years...has been more familiar to more people for a longer period of time than any other place on earth. This is the city of David, who unified the land and proclaimed Jerusalem the capital in the tenth century B.C. This is the city of Solomon's Temple. This is the city of Isaiah and Jeremiah."

"Throughout the centuries of their dispersion, in whatever far corner of the earth they found themselves, the Jews prayed for their return to Zion. Archaeologists and historians have long wondered why Jerusalem should have been established where it was. It enjoyed none of the physical features which favored advancement and prosperity, such as were enjoyed by other important cities in the world. It stood at the head of no great river. It overlooked no great harbor. It commanded no great highway. It possessed no mineral riches. It was off the main trade routes. Yet over it multiple thousands have been slaughtered throughout the centuries. It has been burned and pillaged, wrecked and razed but always to grow again from its own rubble. No other city has so profoundly touched the lives and laws of men. Hundreds of millions who have never seen Jerusalem honor it in thought and in prayer."

"An interesting sidelight for our viewers," Tom interrupted, "while Jerusalem has never stood at the head of a great river... recent events have changed that. As many of you know a stream now runs beneath the Temple area. Right in this area the water is up to one's ankles and just some 5000 feet from here it's impossible to walk across. There are many trees now growing on

Then he brought me back to the door of the house; and behold, water was flowing from under the threshold of the house toward the east, for the house faced east. And the water was flowing down from under, from the right side of the house, from south of the altar.

Now when I had returned, behold, on the bank of the river there were very many trees on the one side and on the other.

both sides of this river. What did you find in the Dead Sea area, Bill?"

"Tom, it's really amazing! This river flows east through the desert into the Jordan Valley and the Dead Sea. In fact the Dead Sea is no longer dead. Many of you who have travelled here remember that the Dead Sea has the earth's lowest surface, 1300 feet below sea level. The salt concentration reached 25%, four times that of ocean water. The magnesium bromide prevented the growth of organic life, and the heat was extreme. In this area God's destruction of Sodom took place."

"But the waters here now are no longer salty. They are fresh and pure. This is a fisherman's paradise because fish abound in this sea! There are all kinds of fish here...and all kinds of fruit

> Then he said to me, "These waters go out toward the eastern region and go down into the Arabah [the valley of the Jordan]; then they go toward the sea, being made to flow into the sea, and the waters of the [Dead] sea become fresh.
>
> And it will come about that every living creature which swarms in every place where the river goes, will live. And there will be very many fish, for these waters go there, and the others become fresh, so everything will live where the river goes.
> (Ezekiel 47:1,7-9 ASV)
>
> And it will come about that fishermen will stand beside it; from Eingedi to Eneglaim there will be a place for the spreading of nets. Their fish will be according to their kinds, like the fish of the Mediterranean Sea, very many.
> (Ezekiel 47:10 ASV)

trees grow along the river banks. We have been told that the leaves will never turn brown and fall!"

"An unusual phenomena, Bill," Tom added, "is that the fruit trees will bear a new crop every month — without fail! These waters flowing from the Temple area have most unusual characteristics...a special blessing of life from God. And the leaves of these trees have already been used for healing. My own wife, Terry, has benefited from this new spiritual medicine."

"An interesting thought." George remarked, "is that in direct contrast to this, the marshes and swamps in the area do not contain fresh water but continue

> And by the river on its bank... will grow all kinds of trees for food... and their leaves for healing.
> (Ezekiel 47:12 ASV)

The Dead Sea is no longer dead. The familiar salt towers have all disappeared!

salty. I wonder if this is a picture of this Millennium Period...that while peace and happiness will prevail in this near-perfect time... we will still be witnessing some conflict."

"Bill, fill our viewers in on the nature of this new Kingdom and on Jerusalem's part in this."

"Thank you, George. As I am sure you know, the world government now is a theocracy. The theocratic rule will center in Jerusalem. This is the center of our Millennial earth. As our television cameras pan the skyline, let's get a shot of the entire area from our blimp overhead. Jerusalem is already much bigger than it ever was before in history. But the city will even be enlarged far beyond its present dimensions. It will never again be destroyed."

"Everyone is now able to come to Jerusalem. There is no need for passports...nor for that matter, innoculations. No baggage inspection. No body frisking. You will find this city completely accessible. Quite a contrast, isn't it from the world of the 1970's and 1980's."

"And, of course, Jerusalem is now the world's center of worship."

George, thought for a moment, then spoke. "Bill, do you know something that all of us Living

But its swamps and marshes will not become fresh; they will be left for salt.
(Ezekiel 47:11 ASV)

...in the last days... the mountain of the Lord's house shall be established in the top of the mountains, and shall be exalted above the hills; and all nations shall flow into it.

And many people shall go and say, Come ye, and let us go up to the mountain of the Lord, to the house of the God of Jacob; and He will teach us in His paths: for out of Zion shall go forth the law and the word of the Lord from Jerusalem.

And He shall judge among the nations, and shall rebuke many people: and they shall beat their swords into plowshares, and their spears into pruning hooks; nation shall not lift up sword against nation, neither shall they learn war any more.
(Isaiah 2:2-4)

All the land will be changed into a plain from Geba [the northern border of Judah] to Rimmon south of Jerusalem; but Jerusalem will rise and remain on its site from Benjamin's gate as far as the place of the First Gate to the Corner Gate, and from the Tower of Hananel to the king's wine presses.

And people will live in it, and there will be no more curse, for Jerusalem will dwell in security.
(Zechariah 14:10-11 ASV)

And an highway shall be there, and a way, and it shall be called The way of holiness; the unclean shall not pass over it;

Believers have taken for granted ...and perhaps didn't realize? And yet it is a major change...so major, some of us failed to recognize it. In fact, I'm amazed, simply amazed. This is a tremendous boon to those of us who are in the television industry... and radio!"

> but it shall be for those: the wayfaring men, though fools, shall not err therein.
>
> No lion shall be there, nor any ravenous beast shall go up thereon, it shall not be found there; but the redeemed shall walk there.
>
> **(Isaiah 35:8-9)**

"What's that, George?" Bill inquired.

"Our languages. We can suddenly understand each other! No more English, French, Spanish, or Russian. A few moments ago I was speaking to some Italians and a couple Israelis and we each understood each other. It never dawned on me that I would need an interpreter."

"That's true, George," Tom added, "you see, so many changes have occurred so rapidly in the past few weeks it's difficult for us to comprehend them all. What we are witnessing is a unified language. Every obstacle to human understanding and international accord has been taken away.

"Think what this will do for world trade...with these barriers removed!"

> For then will I turn to the people a pure language, that they may all call upon the name of the Lord, to serve Him with one consent.
>
> **(Zephaniah 3:9)**

"Right, Tom, but let's describe the scene before us," George continued. "This Temple area is being greatly enlarged as the worship center of the world. Just a moment...David, Regent over all of Palestine, has just made his entrance. Let's go down to the rostrum."

Suddenly everything became quiet. Here was David. George felt shivers run up and down his back. As a Resurrected Believer he had the same glow about him as Helen, Bill and Tom. But his regal robes quickly identified his royal status. Could this be the David born in 1040 B.C., George thought to himself ...the little David that slew Goliath, the Philistine, with a few pebbles; the David who Saul tried to slay; the David who committed adultery with Bath-sheba and murdered her husband to conceal his crime...?

His thoughts were interrupted by David, speaking:

The Lord is my rock and my fortress and my deliverer;
For the waves of death encompassed me;
The torrents of destruction overwhelmed me;
The cords of Sheol surrounded me;
    I cried to my God;
    And from His temple He heard my voice [1]

And I will make an everlasting covenant with you,
According to the faithful mercies shown to David.
Behold, I have made him a witness to the peoples,
    A leader and commander for the peoples. [2]

Strangers shall no longer make Israel their slaves.

But they shall serve the Lord their God, and
David their king, whom I will raise up for them. [3]

David then went into the body of his message:

"In this Millennium Period, our Redeemer King, our Messiah, Jesus Christ, will receive worship. He will not engage in acts of worship. As your Regent the Lord has chosen me to lead in worship. There will be memorial sacrifices...memorials of that perfect sacrifice made by the One typified by all sacrifice, the Lamb of God, that taketh away the sin of the world."

"As you know, those born in this Millennium Period are born in sin. Salvation is still necessary for them to gain access to the coming New Heavens and New Earth. The memorial sacrifice will *not* be a means of salvation. Salvation will wholly be based on the value of the death of Christ and will be appropriated by faith alone even as Abraham appropriated God's promise and was justified.

And without faith it is impossible to please Him, for he who comes to God must believe that He is, and that He is a rewarder of those that seek Him. [4]

For what does the Scripture say? And Abraham believed God, and it was credited to his account as righteousness. [5]

---

[1] 2 Samuel 22:2, 5-7   [3] Jeremiah 30:9   [5] Romans 4:3, quoting Genesis 15:6
[2] Isaiah 55:3-4   [4] Hebrews 11:6

This Worship Center when completed will be a spacious square, 34 miles each way and containing about 1160 square miles. This area will be the center of all divine government and worship and will be readily accessible to all."

George Omega requested permission to address Regent David: "Sir, can you tell us a little about the Temple?"

Regent David replied:

"The Temple will be in an area 8⅓ miles long and 6⅔ miles wide...as written in Ezekiel 48:8.

The Redeemer King has appointed me Regent over all of Palestine...ministering under the authority of Jesus Christ, the King. It will be my duty to divide the land allotted to us.

What you may not realize is that now, for the first time ISRAEL will possess ALL the land promised to Abraham in Genesis 15:18-21."

"We have noticed some changes occurring, sir...what will these land changes mean?"

The topography of the land will soon be altered. Mountainous terrain will soon all disappear.

David again spoke, saying,

"The topography of the land, its features, have been greatly altered. Mountainous terrain has all but disappeared. A great fertile plain has come into existence.

Even as prophesied in Isaiah 35:7 and 51:3 there will be renewed fertility.

And rain...there will be an abundance of rain.[1]

Rain will become a blessing...and its withholding will be a penalty for those who refuse to honor God.[2]

Land will be reconstructed throughout the world because of the ravages of the period of tribulation.[3]

And Palestine will be redistributed among the 12 tribes of Israel within the next few days.[4]

ISRAEL IS ONCE AGAIN REUNITED AS A NATION!

In those days the house of Judah will walk with the house of Israel, and they will come together from the land of the north to the land that I gave your fathers as an inheritance."

"This is George Omega, bringing to a close our special telecast from Jerusalem. Regent David closed his short message to those assembled in the Temple area with a quotation from the Old Testament, Jeremiah 3:18. Its significance — Israel is back in their land...united...the fulfillment of prophecy...to the letter!"

"If I may add just a word, George, so that our viewers will understand the make-up of this new government?"

"Go right ahead, Tom."

"David is Regent over Palestine in this 1000 year Millennium Period. But he will have nobles and governors reigning under him. These subordinate rulers, working under David, will exercise the theocratic power and

> And their leader shall be one of them, And their ruler shall come forth from their midst; And I will bring him near, and he shall approach Me....
> (Jeremiah 30:21 ASV)
>
> Behold a king will reign righteously, And princes will rule justly.
> (Isaiah 32:1 ASV)

---

[1] Isaiah 30:23
[2] Zechariah 14:17
[3] Isaiah 61:4-5; Ezekiel 36:33-35
[4] Ezekiel 48:1-29

administer the government. But it must also be kept in mind that there will be also lesser authorities who will rule as well. Quite a description of this is found in Luke 19:12-18. Many of them will rule over a block of 15 cities throughout Israel, being responsible to the head of the tribe, who, in turn will be responsible to David. And, of course, Regent David is responsible to the Redeemer King Himself. These appointments have been made to certain Resurrected Believers as a reward for their previous faithfulness during their earthly lives."

"One other thing...we will soon be witnessing the appointment of many judges. This reign is universal, covering the entire earth. This same subdivided authority will be found in the United States, in Australia, in Africa... everywhere. So you see, we finally have a unified world government...but one under the authority of our Lord and Saviour."

> **And I will restore thy judges as at the first, and thy counsellors as at the beginning: afterward thou shalt be called, The city of righteousness, the faithful city.**
>
> **(Isaiah 1:26)**

> **And there was given Him dominion, and glory, and a kingdom, that all people, nations, and languages, should serve Him: His dominion is an everlasting dominion, which shall not pass away, and His kingdom that which shall not be destroyed.**
>
> **And the kingdom and dominion, and the greatness of the kingdom under the whole heaven, shall be given to the people of the saints of the most High, whose kingdom is an everlasting kingdom, and all dominions shall serve and obey Him.**
>
> **(Daniel 7:14,27)**

* * *

It had been an exciting day and George looked forward to going home to his apartment to see Helen, Sue and Tommy. Upon arriving he found Sylvia there as well as Faye and Terry.

For a period that was supposed to be happy, Sylvia and Terry never seemed to reflect it.

"George!" Sylvia exclaimed, "I just came back from the Judge's office on Nablus Road. I asked him what happened to Carole Sutherland in the judgment of the Gentiles in the Valley of Jehoshaphat. George, George...she's been sent to Hades. She never made it, George. She never made it! What will we tell Harry?"

George whitened. A feeling of revolt stirred within him. It hadn't all been settled...this Millennium. Somehow George felt that the turmoil within him would one day explode. He could not control his anger as he spoke.

"Why Carole? Why did God have to do this to Carole? She seemed so good. She attended church even more than Harry. Why not Harry? I never knew Harry was a Christian...but Carole ...she always spoke religious...counted out her tithe every Sunday...observed Lent...everything. She lived the life!"

Helen started to speak, but Sue interrupted.

"Daddy, Christ saved us not according to our works but by His grace. Don't you remember Ephesians 2:8-9...*By grace are ye saved through faith.* That's the key word, Daddy, FAITH. It is the GIFT of God. That's another key word, Daddy, **GIFT.** It's not something we can achieve on our own by money or by doing good deeds or by living a good life. To spend an eternity with God in heaven means we must accept His GIFT. Verse 9 tells us it is NOT OF WORKS. So many people fail to understand such a simple verse. Its simplicity becomes a stumbling stone for them. We must accept reality. They were wrong, those who used to claim that every religion is good and that no matter what road you travelled you would get to Heaven. This was FALSE. It simply was not true. Nowhere in the Bible was such a statement ever made. In fact Matthew 7:13-14 says just the opposite:

> Enter in at the narrow gate;
>> for wide is the gate,
>> and broad is the way
>> that leadeth to destruction,
>> and many there be who go in that way;
> Because narrow is the gate,
>> and hard is the way,
>> which leadeth unto life
>> and few there be that find it.

But many people don't bother to read the Scriptures. They go on making up their own ideas of what the Bible says. Then when judgment comes...oh, do they cry and plead...but it's too late ...too late, Daddy!"

No more trash problems. The slum areas had disappeared.

Helen tried to soften Sue's comments: "George, you are now seeing first hand the reality of judgment. And it hurts. I can understand. But how often has there been sorrow in Heaven... God gave His Son on Calvary to redeem man...but man remained so engulfed in a race for material gains...that he ignored the gift; and by so ignoring God's free gift of life, he remained condemned in his sins. That's what Carole did!"

* * *

It wasn't easy for George to pick up the phone and call Harry Sutherland. How could he break the news? If it happened in the 1970's and Carole had died in some accident...at least George could comfort Harry with the wishful thought that she was in Heaven and soon he would see her there.

But this was not the 1970's...nor the 1980's.

And he could offer Harry no hope. It was beyond that. All he could say was that Carole was judged at the Valley of Jehoshaphat...and while in the milling multitude of millions... Harry passed through the right gate, Carole was ushered through the left gate and escorted by a cordon of guards to Hades to await eternal punishment in the Lake of Fire.

And that's exactly what he told Harry when the phone connection was finally established.

But all Harry could reply as though hypnotized in horror was: "No hope...no hope...for an eternity...oh my...no hope!"

* * *

The months passed quickly. In that time George had flown several times back to New York. It was a new city. No more air pollution. No more trash problems. No more abandoned cars. No more crime. The slum areas had disappeared and there was no more art for art's sake or scientific energies wasted on improving liquor qualities. All that which was once foolishly spent had suddenly been turned for world improvement. What many

...In the day that I shall have cleansed you from all your iniquities I will also cause you to dwell in the cities, and the wastes shall be builded.
(Ezekiel 36:33)

Behold, the days come, saith the Lord, that the plowman shall overtake the reaper, and

Presidents had aspired for...a "Great Society"...was now a reality.

Even wars had been eliminated.

No wonder such progress could take place. George remembered how in the 1970's the United States budget was some $250 billion. Of this, $78 billion was spent for defense and even $1 billion for flood relief. This was no longer necessary. No wars... no need for a defense budget nor arms. No hazards such as floods, fires, auto accidents...no need for relief budgets. Psalm 91 was at last a reality.

> the treader of grapes him that soweth seed; and the mountains shall drop sweet wine, and all the hills shall be dissolved.
>
> (Amos 9:13)
>
> And I will cut off the chariot from Ephraim, And the horse from Jerusalem; And the bow of war will be cut off. And He will speak peace to the nations; And His dominion will be from sea to sea, And from the River to the ends of the earth.
>
> (Zechariah 9:10 ASV)
>
> They shall not hurt nor destroy in all my holy mountain: for the earth shall be full of the knowledge of the LORD, as the waters cover the sea.
>
> (Isaiah 11:9)

Billions of dollars were no longer needed to run the United States Government. When a semblance of peace came in January, 1973 in Vietnam, Dr. Henry Kissinger had a staff of over 100 people. In 3 years time, from 1969 to 1972 the cost of running the White House doubled from $31 million to $71 million.

And working under the President at that time were 2.8 million people, drawing some $32 billion a year in salaries — *double* that of 10 years earlier in 1962!

The nation was in a Trillion dollar economy and yet it had empty pockets!

In fact, in the early 1970's, social welfare spending of all kinds by all levels of government in the U.S. topped $160 billion... and more than half of all the money American taxpayers paid went for that purpose.

But that was all in the past. These billions of dollars would no longer be wasted in man's

> And they shall build houses, and inhabit them; and they shall plant vinyards, and eat the fruit of them.
>
> They shall not build, and another inhabit; they shall not plant, and another eat: for as the days of a tree are the days of my people, and mine elect shall long enjoy the work of their hands.

puny efforts to erect a great society.

The 1000 year Millennium Age had changed all that. No more social welfare was needed. No

They shall not labour in vain, nor bring forth for trouble; for they are the seed of the blessed of the Lord, and their offspring with them.

(Isaiah 65:21-23)

more government control was needed. No more peace envoys flitting back and forth from Hanoi to Paris and from Washington to Paris.

Monies once foolishly wasted were now being directed towards a perfect industrialized society under the direct guidance of the Redeemer King. Everyone was able to work now. And everyone's needs could be met. We were living in an age of economic prosperity.

* * *

Faye suddenly awoke. She felt a strange stirring within her. It was the 9th month of her pregnancy...yet the pains normally accompanying an impending birth were not there. She was not worried. She remembered her doctor told her to drink Chamomile tea every night in her ninth month. How she treasured the promise of Ezekiel 47:12...

...their leaves for healing.

These leaves from the river bank off the fruit trees...growing where once there was a Dead Sea...now were eliminating the pain of childbirth.

Long ago in England the true chamomile was recognized by its flower and its important healing blue oil. It blossomed from May to October and the leaves were dried for tea. The tea was an aid to digestion and had a soothing, cleansing, anti-spasmodic effect. And now God had perfected this leaf for healing.

And although the pains were not there...she knew it was time to go to the hospital. She was alone at the time. George had gone over to check on Terry and Sylvia about an upcoming telecast.

Faye quickly picked up the phone, dialing Terry's apartment.

"George, oh I'm so glad to hear your voice. Can you come over, quick. I'm going to have my baby."

"Hold on," George gasped, "Terry is also going to have her's.

She's in labor. I'll get in the car and be right over. Keep calm, Faye, honey, keep calm. I'll be there quickly!"

It was like a family reunion in the hospital.

Bill beamed at Faye. He was so proud of her. And Faye was like a breath of springtime...holding her treasured possession ...a baby girl.

"What shall we name her, honey?" Bill asked.

"I would like to name her, Esther. I believe great things are in store for her, Bill. She won't become Queen of Persia, but I believe God will use her in a mighty way."

* * *

Tom Malone sat on Terry's bed. Terry was beaming. It was one of the few times Tom had seen her so radiant.

But why shouldn't she be. In her arms was a cuddly boy. Doctors had been afraid for a moment that the child was to be born blind...but a healing leaf applied to his eyelids at birth brought immediate sight.

"What will we name him, darling?" Tom asked as he kissed her gently.

"Let's call him, Bart."

"Fine, a short version of Bartimaeus...the blind man healed by Jesus as he went out from Jericho on His way to Jerusalem... wonderful...so true to our own experience! Fine, we'll call him Bart!"

Esther and Bart.

What did the future hold for them?

The Millennium was to be 1000 years of peace!

But for Esther and Bart it would also be filled with trials and tragedy.

Chapter 6

MARRIAGE at MEGIDDO

Bart Malone had reached his 48th birthday. And the Malones, the Omegas, and the Sanders decided to throw a surprise party ...not only for Bart but also for Esther Sanders.

Terry was concerned for Bart. While setting up the decorations she questioned George.

"I don't understand Bart lately, George. In just a few days his whole attitude towards life appears to have changed. I thought your offer of having him help you at World Television Network would be a tremendous outlet for his talents. I may be prejudiced, I know, but I've never met anyone like Bart, who is so discerning and so capable of handling many jobs."

"Terry, Bart took to the task like a fish to water. He loves television and is an excellent researcher. He shows a particular interest in the events of the Tribulation Period. It seems as if he's asked me a thousand questions on our experiences during that time. I thought he was coming along fine. I guess that's why I took him to the Temple area the other day for an open court hearing. But even I was surprised...and I must admit, a little dismayed."

"What happened, George? You never told me."

"A man was brought to Regent David who was caught short-weighing groceries in his store and pumping his meats with water to gain more profits. It seemed rather ridiculous since food is so much in abundance, and there is want of nothing. But there's always someone who wants to make more. I guess the real reason for his arrest was his threat to kill the lady who exposed his manipulations."

"What's this have to do with Bart?"

"Bart and I covered the judging of this case. Bart and I both thought this would be a routine case. It was the first case on the docket for Jerusalem that morning. That's the only reason we found it worthwhile to be there with our TV cameras. We assumed a slap on the wrist by the judge, a warning, would be the crux of the whole thing."

"Was it?" Terry anxiously inquired.

"No, that's just it. The judge heard the case with Regent David. Regent David then simply said...

All those plotting evil will be killed.
He will strike the earth with the rod of His mouth,
And with the breath of His lips He will slay the wicked. [1]

And with that the poor rascal was literally blown to bits as though a laser beam had struck him. Poof...vanished!"

"Then what happened?"

"I tried to report it matter-of-factly but I'm sure Bart sensed the shock in my voice at so swift a judgment. Later, as we drove back to the studio, Bart let me have it...

'I don't understand this, Mr. Omega. This is supposed to be the Millennium...where there's peace and love. You told me that Brother Bartholomew used the laser ring to exercise his power over man. Frankly I can't see any difference here. This man didn't kill anyone. Sure, he tried to make a few extra dollars. Why couldn't he have been detained or put on a special work force. And if God is so omnipotent and perfect, what happened to His perfect work? You know sir, I think someone is being sold a bill of goods!'

And I saw an angel come down from heaven, having the key to the bottomless pit and a great chain in his hand.

And he laid hold on the dragon, that old serpent which is the Devil, and Satan, and bound him a thousand years,

And cast him into the bottomless pit, and shut him up, and set a seal upon him, that he should deceive the nations no more, till the thousand years should be fulfilled: and after that he must be loosed a little season.

(Revelation 20:1-3)

[1] Isaiah 29:20 and 11:4.

I tried to explain to Bart that even in the Millennium there will be some who will rebel even though Satan has been bound for these 1000 years in the Bottomless Pit. But you know, Bart has a mind of his own. And nothing I could say would satisfy him."

"I'm sorry, George, so sorry. Let's pray for Bart, that he will see the foolishness of his ways. I'm sure Esther will have an influence on him. They've been seeing a lot of each other lately. They're so young...only 48 and already I've overheard them talking about marriage."

* * *

It was a real family reunion. The Resurrected Believers who were present included Helen Omega, Sue and Tommy, along with Bill Sanders and Tom Malone. The Living Believers included George Omega, Faye Sanders, Terry Malone, Sylvia Epstein, and Harry and Phil Sutherland, who had both flown in from New York.

Phil Sutherland was Harry's nephew, a tall, handsome mustached man, with wavy, jet black hair. He had recently been promoted to a Vice-Presidential slot at World Television Network's New York main office. He was 45, a millennial child, young, up and coming, and on the move. Everyone, especially the ladies, loved him.

When Bart and Esther walked in holding hands...everyone shouted "SURPRISE" and it was a real surprise. Blushingly they went around kissing each one and whispering a thank you.

Harry broke the ice: "Well you youngsters have finally reached 48. You know, back in our days we thought 48 was middle age. But everything is different in this Millennial Age. Why you're just teenagers! How does it feel to be grown up?"

> No longer will there be in it an infant who lives but a few days, Or an old man who does not live out his days; For the youth will die at the age of one hundred And the one who does not reach the age of one hundred Shall be brought accursed [a rebellious sinner].
>
> **(Isaiah 65:20 ASV)**

"Great, Harry, just great," Bart replied.

The spread was unbelievable. All kinds of foods and fruits

that would tempt the most sluggish appetite. Oranges as big as grapefruit, seedless, easy to peel and succulently sweet... lemons a rosy pink, larger than pre-millennial oranges. Not bitter, not sweet...a hollow bamboo shoot thrust into the lemon served as a straw. It took the place of soft drinks. One lemon producing a full glass of juice...juice "so heavenly" as George often remarked, that "It's the drink of Resurrected Believers!" It was a real thirst quencher.

Faye was talking to Terry, "I've never had so much fun. No more weight watching...no more counting calories. It's like heaven here. We can eat anything. Joy, oh what perfect joy!"

> Thou shalt multiply the nation, Thou shalt increase their gladness; They will be glad in Thy presence As with the gladness of harvest, As men rejoice when they divide the spoil.
>
> **(Isaiah 9:3 ASV)**

Terry's face turned from a smile to sudden concern as she noticed Bart and Esther huddled in a corner talking excitedly.

Esther, like a gift from Heaven, her body so beautifully proportioned, had long hair shimmering in golden tresses over her shoulders. Terry sensed not just an outward beauty...but an inner beauty. Esther was soft-spoken almost to the point of retiring, yet firm in her convictions and in her testimony for God. There was no compromising with Esther. And though she was aware of her desirability among men...she had more than once told Bart she believed in the purity of marriage.

Bart, young and aggressive, found this hard to understand. And in light of what he believed was unfair judgment at the Temple area, his sense of balance was becoming unhinged.

Bart almost embarrassingly held Esther tightly in his arms. He hoped the relative darkness of the corner near the drapes would hide his actions and muffle the sounds of agitated conversation.

"Esther, honey, I love you. I need you. I can't go on living this way. Life is just becoming too complicated. We've been dating now for 10 years...ever since we've been 38. Let's get married."

"Bart, I love you, too. But there's so much to consider...Mom and Mrs. Malone and Uncle George and Daddy. Have you asked your father?"

"What communication can my father and I have? He's a resurrected believer!"

"That doesn't mean anything, Bart, you can talk to him."

"Esther, are you so blind that you can't see the hurt in my mother's eyes? Sure she can talk to him...but that's all!"

"But...Bart..." Esther tried to continue realizing that a real gulf did exist between Living and Resurrected Believers...a gulf that would not be totally resolved until after the Millennial Period.

"Honey, five years ago, I gave you an engagement ring. I don't think it's unreasonable to get married now...even next month...please darling, please. Things are just falling apart with me. If I don't have you, I don't know what will happen. You should have been at the Temple area when that judgment took place. I'm concerned, Esther, concerned...and I just can't go it alone anymore. I need you, Esther. I need you!"

For the first time in her life Esther saw Bart cry. Tears etched their way down his rugged face. He tried to hold them back... but they welled up in his eyes and like a burst dam, suddenly overflowing. At first Bart pretended they weren't there as he buried his face in her lap. Esther, understandingly, took out her favorite orchid handkerchief which Bart had given her on their first date, and gently wiped away the tears.

She kissed the lobe of his ear and whispered, "Everything will be alright, Bart...please don't cry...I will marry you...next month ...and you can announce that right now!"

Bart beamed as he kissed Esther. No other words were spoken. That kiss expressed what words could never tell.

Bart, partially to regain his composure and stop the flow of tears walked over to young Phil Sutherland, the bright and aggressive tall nephew of Harry Sutherland. Bart wanted to change the subject...anything to halt the moisture in his eyes. Then, too, now that marriage was just around the corner, he wanted to firm up his job with Phil who had just recently been named as a new Vice President at World Television Net-

"Everything will be alright, Bart...I will marry you."

work. After all, Bart thought, as a husband, I'm going to have added responsibilities.

Phil was glad to get to know him. Doubts also had been creeping into Phil's mind about the whole Millennium Period, and from some of the remarks he overheard Bart make, Phil sensed he would find a sympathizer in Bart.

"Mr. Sutherland, sir, I hope to get married soon and, well, I just wondered. You know Mr. Omega has been using me in the area of research for his telecasts. Do you think it will be permanent, sir? Will I have a chance to travel and see world activities first hand?"

"Tell me, Bart," Phil Sutherland asked, in what appeared to be a change of the subject, "what did you think of the Judgment at the Temple area the other day?"

"Frankly speaking sir, I was very upset. Well, I just thought it to be unfair. I felt that the judgment was very harsh. It got me to thinking, sir...."

This was the answer Phil Sutherland had hoped to hear. At last someone was thinking like himself.

"Bart, don't worry, there's a permanent job for you at World Television Network. Both George Omega and my uncle Harry have been telling me of your unusual depth in news coverage and of your recent research on Brother Bartholomew."

"Yes, sir, he must have been a very fascinating man. Don't misunderstand me...not that I admire him...but to have gained so much power in so short a time. I feel as though I actually knew him. Crazy thought, I know."

"Not so crazy as one would imagine. Often in researching an individual as extensively as you have...one almost gets to know him...almost to know him as one's own father. And in this knowing, we sometimes can understand a man's actions and why he did the things he did."

"I guess you're right, Mr. Sutherland," and then, seeking to dismiss the subject, "but, sir, I feel like I'm sitting on top of the world...ready to get married. I'd like to spend my honeymoon in New York City. I've never been there...and I've read so much about it. First, we'll get married right here in Jerusalem, of course."

"Of course, Bart, in Jerusalem," Phil interrupted. "But may I make a suggestion about that?"

"Sure, sir, sure." A blush came over Bart's face, as he realized how quickly he was making a hit with his new boss...and yet Phil's thinking and his seemed to run in the same patterns and he felt sudden kinship.

Phil, beckoned him closer, so he could talk in a whisper, unheard by anyone.

"Bart, a thought just occurred to me. Jerusalem has been so much in the news these past 50-odd years...and your wedding is going to be an important event. I just hate to see it overshadowed by some judgment or other that may occur on the same day...demanding TV coverage."

"Yes, Mr. Sutherland."

"Phil will be fine, Bart. Just call me Phil."

"Fine, Phil."

With this Phil Sutherland continued to reveal his new thoughts to Bart, saying, "What area in Palestine, besides Jerusalem has real news significance...digging back in past history? You've done plenty of research...what area do you think, Bart?"

"I'm not sure, Phil."

"You were just talking of Brother Bartholomew. Where were his achievements climaxed?"

"Megiddo, at the Battle of Armageddon...the Plain of Esdraelon."

"Precisely...and what better place to hold your wedding than at Megiddo!"

"But why there?"

"Just this...Megiddo has long been remembered for its evil. Now, you and Esther, will unite in marriage there...each having one parent who is a Resurrected Believer and one parent who is a Living Believer. It will be a TV triumph...like the old soap operas...a triumph over injustice.

We can promote it as the MARRIAGE AT MEGIDDO. It will be the culmination of all things good!"

"Excellent idea, Phil...never thought of it that way. Boy, will Esther be thrilled!"

"May I make a suggestion, Bart...why not let Esther announce your impending marriage and you then announce the location. It will be a doubleheader surprise."

About five minutes later Phil Sutherland stood before everyone waving his arms. His voice assumed a pretended formality as he said, "May we have your attention, everyone...Bart Malone and Esther Sanders have a couple of announcements."

Esther stood sheepishly in front of the whole family gathering. Everyone was quiet. She smiled as she prepared to speak...

"Bart asked me to make an announcement...and then he'll make an announcement that even I don't know. As you know Bart and I have been engaged for 5 years. Now we believe it is the Lord's will that we be married...within the month. And we're so happy!"

Shouts of joy and congratulations filled the room. Sylvia, between the tears kissed Esther and said, "I'm so happy, I'm crying." And soon Esther was surrounded by Faye and Terry Malone who, in turn, then hugged Bart.

Bart hushed the audience and stood next to Esther, his arm

tightly around her waist...he then gently kissed her on the forehead and began his speech.

"I hope you are ready for another surprise. We were thinking of getting married in Jerusalem. In fact, that's what Esther and I had talked about. But I have a surprise for all of you...including Esther. It may strike you as unusual at first...but I am sure it will be a blessing for all of us. Phil Sutherland gave me the idea. And I think it's great."

"Quit holding us in suspense," George interjected. "Where's the wedding going to be held?"

Bart straightened up, put on his biggest smile and continued: "The wedding will take place in MEGIDDO. Think of it...a MARRIAGE AT MEGIDDO!"

Bart's attention was suddenly drawn to his mother. It was as though something he had said had suddenly enveloped her in tragedy.

She let out a small "ohhh" and collapsed in the arms of Faye Sanders.

Why did mother have to be so emotional, he thought. What was to be a happy occasion had quickly changed its focus.

And Bart was disturbed.

* * *

To get Bart's mind off the impending marriage and to give Esther time to get ready for this event, Harry Sutherland, his nephew Phil—the new V.P.—and George Omega all got together and decided that Bart should join Phil and George in a news expedition to Egypt.

"Why Egypt?" Bart inquired.

"Egypt is stirring," Phil replied.

"And when anyone stirs...we're there." George continued. "You see the rulers of Egypt are disenchanted with the theocratic type of government emanating from Jerusalem. Some of the old bitterness of Arab-Israeli conflict still lingers. Some say it initially

> But thou, Bethlehem Ephratah, though thou be little among the thousands of Judah, yet out of thee shall He come forth unto Me that is to be ruler in Israel; whose goings forth have been from of old, from everlasting.
>
> **(Micah 5:2)**

was triggered by the shooting down of the Libyan passenger jet by the Israeli's in February, 1973 killing over 100 people and the subsequent Black September reprisal in Sudan of two U.S. diplomats. We don't know if this is simply talk in the wind or whether we will see some sort of uprising. This trip will give you a good time for research...in case some conflict arises."

Bart remarked, "Everyone knows that Christ in the Millennium has been given absolute power to govern."

"Not only that," Phil interjected, "but Gentiles as well as Israelis must submit to the authority of Christ. This may be hard for some to accept...this theocratic authority. And I suppose, most difficult for those in Egypt and other Arabic countries ...who now see the promises going in the direction of the nation of Israel; particularly Palestine's enlarged territory!"

> **All the ends of the world shall remember and turn unto the Lord: and all the kindreds of the nations shall worship before thee.**
>
> **For the kingdom is the Lord's: and He is the governor among the nations.**
>
> **(Psalm 22:27-28)**

* * *

Cairo was resplendent in color when the trio of Phil, George, and Bart arrived. It no longer experienced the Khamsin...the wind that lays a tapestry of sand and dust across the skyline.

This was the Millennial Earth and Cairo was a part of it. Cairo had been a city of much suffering through 2000 years. No more were women carrying incredible cargoes on their heads. Produce and other forms of commerce were abundant. Both Cairo University and the once-Islamic Al Azhar were now engaged in practical training that would equip its young men and women for productive work in this enlightened age.

Cairo...once in the dregs of poverty...was finally, in reality the "Garden of the world"...a name the historian Ibn Khaldun had called it in the 14th century.

The familiar Sphinx and the Pyramids were still being repaired from the damage which they sustained during the Tribulation earthquakes. There was a friendliness everywhere in the streets...joyful reunions as men greeted relatives with *"Ya habibi, ya habibi"* — My sweetheart, my sweetheart. More

No more were women carrying incredible cargoes on their heads.

shouting followed: *"Souma, Souma,"* and *"Ya qalbi"* — My heart.

The Arabs were a warm-hearted, friendly people. Too often they had been misunderstood in the 1960's to 1980's. What many did not realize is that it takes a lot to make an Arab angry. Often this tenderness is interpreted as cowardice.

George Omega laughingly remarked: "I recall reading about Dr. Youssef Idris' strategy for defeating Israel in the 1970's."

"Idris had said,

> 'We'll get all 34 million Egyptians together and march them to the Suez Canal. On a given signal, when we are face-to-face with the enemy, all 34 million of us will smile. Are you aware of how disarming it would be to look on 34 million smiling Egyptians?'"

"Dr. Idris had a point, didn't he?" George chuckled.

Bart was particularly impressed with the rich oriental rugs... the hammered copper plates...the ornate brass trays...and the deeply satisfying Turkish coffee.

Soon they arrived at Abdin Palace, in the center of Cairo. It was from here where Abdel Nasser and Anwar Sadat once ruled their country. But all that was yesterday. What seemed important then...was now merely a memory...no longer of any significance...the trials...the struggles...the tribulations...all forgotten; surpassed by the over flowing light of the Millennial years.

Hassan Ahmed was now Governor of Egypt. He had high aspirations upon his appointment. The Palace was beautiful. The walls were heavy with masterpieces of art. The sparkle of crystal was everywhere. One of the baths even had walls of salmon-colored alabaster.

While this was the Millennial Age...none of the customs and traditions which were genuinely Arabic had changed...yet, with an old Arabic word thrown in periodically for flavor, all spoke the universal language. This in itself broke down barriers of difference.

As George Omega interviewed Governor Ahmed, it was ap-

The Arabs were a warm hearted, friendly people. Too often they had been misunderstood in the 1960's to 1980's.

parent to Bart that all chose their words carefully.

"Sir, I understand that there have been some rumors, some rumblings about, shall I say, 'being under the yoke of Israel.' Are these old hatreds still evident?"

"How should I answer you...yes or no? This is the Millennial Age. We strive for perfection. We are blessed with full knowledge.

> And all thy children shall be taught of the LORD; and great shall be the peace of thy children.
> (Isaiah 54:13)

There is no comparison in this Age with the tragedies of the Tribulation Period. What a difference! The curse has been removed...as promised in Isaiah, chapter 11, verses 6 to 9, the wolf and the lamb lie down together. Quite a picture of Israel and her Arab cousins, wouldn't you say?"

"Egypt, Syria, Jordan and our brothers in Lebanon, who have had many injustices...have now seen justice take effect. But there are still problems. And to those of us who lived during those

> He will not be disheartened or crushed, Until He has established justice in the earth; And the coastlands will wait expectantly for His law.
> (Isaiah 42:4 ASV)

Tribulation years...some cannot forget so easily. Our children born since then ask questions. They want answers. Sometimes our answers do not satisfy them. They all do not understand this new theocracy. Some of them do not have this same love and devotion for God that we have. Some even want to go back to 622 A.D. and revive Mohammed. Some still search for Mecca. Some still climb to a small cave among the rocks of Mount Hira to spend days in fasting and meditation."

Then, holding up a poster, as if to bolster his argument, Ahmed continued.

IT IS HE [ALLAH] WHO HAS SENT . . .
AN APOSTLE FROM AMONG THEMSELVES . . .

"Look at this! We are finding these throughout the city of Cairo."

"What does it mean?" Harry questioned.

"It reads like this:

IT IS HE [ALLAH] WHO HAS SENT
AN APOSTLE FROM AMONG THEMSELVES.

"How will this problem be resolved?" George Omega queried.

"I fear for trouble," Ahmed hesitatingly replied. "That's why it is hard for me to give you straight answers. An early Arabic poem perhaps capsules the devil-may-care attitude of these who rebel. It goes:

With the sword I will wash my shame away,
Let God's doom bring on me what it may!

Yes, I fear trouble. I don't know what Regent David will do, and I myself don't know what to do."

The interview ended. Bart had been greatly impressed. Somehow inside he admired the rebellious attitude that was erupting. He tried to ask himself why. But he could come up with no answers.

The trio of George Omega, Phil Sutherland, and Bart were quiet on their way home. Phil mentioned that perhaps some were getting tired of such quick judgments in Jerusalem. Perhaps, he thought outloud...a harsh theocracy...in spite of its many benefits was not quite the answer.

It was then that Bart spoke... much to the amazement of everyone.

> In that day there will be inscribed on the bells of the horses, "HOLY TO THE LORD." And the cooking pots in the Lord's house will be like the bowls before the altar.
>
> And every cooking pot in Jerusalem and in Judah will be holy to the Lord of hosts; and all who sacrifice will come and take of them and boil in them. And there will be no longer a Canaanite [grasping traders] in the house of the Lord of hosts in that day.
>
> (Zechariah 14:20-21 ASV)

"I think you're right, Phil. People are getting tired of having religion stuffed down their throat. Even the bells on the horses have written on them 'These are Holy Property.' And if that isn't enough...even the trash cans in the Temple area are as holy as the bowls at the altar. That's just going too far!"

* * *

What was once a sprawling kibbutz was now a beautiful plain

dotted with occasional homes and abundant farm land. The communal farms of yesterday were gone. The kibbutzim, perhaps necessary in their time, tended to break the family unity, and they disappeared in the late 1980's. No longer did the dreaded *sharav*...that mass of oven-hot air...plague the area. And the readiness of Nehemiah 4:17.

> ...every one with one of his hands
>   wrought in the work,
> and with the other
>   hand held a weapon.

was no longer necessary in this Millennial Age.

This was the area of Megiddo...once linking Gaza and Damascus and controlling the principal pass through the Carmel range, connecting the coastal plain and the Plain of Esdraelon.

It was here by the waters of Megiddo (Judges 5:19) that Israelite forces under Deborah and Barak annihilated the army of Sisera. It was here that Josiah, the last righteous king of Judah ...before the disintegration of the southern kingdom 586 B.C.... was hit by Egyptian archers and soon died (2 Kings 23:29-30).

And this area...scene of the world's most bitter battle...the Battle of Armageddon...was to become the site of a holy union in marriage.

* * *

Esther Sanders—daughter of Faye and Bill Sanders, granddaughter of George Omega—was a vision of ethereal beauty in her flowing wedding gown. The fingertip veil of illusion made her a vision of loveliness. The gown was floor length of white velvet, with Venice lace trim. It was fashioned with a high neckline and bishop sleeves. Her flowers were red and white carnations with white rosebuds on a white Bible with white ribbon streamers.

George Omega brought the commentary via World Television Network. It was most difficult for him...for this was his family. He recalled the struggle for life itself when not too many years ago his own daughter, Faye, and her husband, Bill, sought to escape the ever-seeking grasp of Brother Bartholomew...the tragedy when Bill met his death on BB's guillotine. Those

"Here on the Plain of Esdraelon...where once millions fought in a battle against the Lord...here you have just witnessed a MARRIAGE AT MEGIDDO!"

memories...so vivid and so real...those events seemed so important then...but God had softened those memories...and transformed them into blessings in this Millennial Age. But somehow, it was difficult for George to choke back the tears. Now...some 50 years later...Faye's daughter and Terry's son were getting married. He thought within himself of an old poem,

> The stately ship is seen no more
> The fragile skiff attains the shore
> And while the great and wise decay
> And all their trophies pass away
> Those found in Christ, in peace sublime
> Still float above the wrecks of Time.

He glanced down at Terry Malone, the groom's mother. This should be her happiest day. And yet he sensed a twinge of sadness...something he just couldn't put his finger on.

George ended his television coverage: "Here, on the Plain of Esdraelon...where once millions fought in a battle against the Lord...here now, where once Armageddon was a word of terror and of judgment...here is love, here is marriage, here is beauty in our Redeemer King. You have just witnessed a MARRIAGE AT MEGIDDO!"

Terry thought to herself...George, I pray you're not wrong ...but I feel we will yet witness a terror beyond our wildest beliefs. She bowed her head..."Please let it not be Esther and Bart...please,...please!"

Their small boat rocked very slowly in the middle of the Sea of Galilee. It was easy to see Bart was in love...All the heartaches... the misunderstandings...Terry's tears at Megiddo were a thing of the past, Esther thought.

Chapter 7

TO LICK THE DUST

Esther had persuaded Bart not to choose New York as their honeymoon site...but rather Galilee.

It was to be their last moment of real happiness...although neither suspected what was ahead.

Bart, who prided himself on his ability to recall events of history, fascinated Esther with his almost photographic memory.

Their small boat rocked very slowly in the middle of the Sea of Galilee. The warmth of the sun...the gentle breezes made a perfect setting for their honeymoon.

No longer was the Sea a polluted waste as it had become in the 1970's. It was again the crystal clear...and this time...quiet Sea that was so evident in the days of Christ's ministry prior to His crucifixion.

It was easy to see that Bart was in love. He stretched out on the boat and laid his head upon Esther's lap. Playfully she ran her finger up and down his nose, around his ears...and when he talked too much...across his lips...sealing it with a kiss.

All the heartaches...the misunderstandings...Terry's tears at Megiddo, were a thing of the past, Esther thought. Bart and I are married now. We're both Christians...at least I know that I am and I am almost certain that Bart is. Nothing can come between us. Ahead of us is continual happiness.

Bart broke the silence: "Honey there's an old Jewish sage who said:

> Jehovah hath created seven seas
> but the Sea of Galilee is His delight.

That man knew what he was talking about."

For Bart and Esther...this was a honeymoon to be remembered. To them there was no fairer sight in all Israel than the view from the Sea of Galilee...with its waters of sapphire blue. Bart reminded Esther that this lake had at one time been called the Sea of Kinneret because it was shaped like a *kinnor* (harp).

Bart continued, "Josephus, concerning this region, said,"

> ...its nature is wonderful as well as its beauty;
> its soil is so fruitful that all sorts of trees can
> grow upon it."

"And the Talmud of old said that the fruit here ripens as fast as deer can run and that one could eat a hundred pieces of it and still wish for more."

"Hush, you walking encyclopedia, this is no time for a history lesson. This is a time for sweet words of gentle love."

For the rest of the afternoon, for Bart and Esther, those gentle words of love came easy.

* * *

For both of them the honeymoon ended too quickly. As they entered Jerusalem there appeared to be great confusion. The native Jews were being almost mobbed by anxious men and women visitors from all over the world. It was as though these tourists were hanging onto the coat sleeves of the citizens of Jerusalem.

"What's going on, honey?" Esther asked.

Bart went over and talked to a bystander and then returned.

"The people of Israel are the VIP's of the Millennium Period. Suddenly they've been transformed from a curse to a blessing. Once prisoners of hope...they are

As for you also, because of the blood of My covenant with you, I have set your prisoners free from the waterless pit.

Return to the stronghold, O

now the object of God's fulfilled promises."

"This is their October festival, I was told. In the old days it was one of mourning. Now it's one of joy. And everyone throughout the world sends representatives to come and worship at the Temple. The Jews are the 'apple of His eye' now and, in my opinion, it becomes a status symbol to enter the Temple with a Jew. That's why you see so many hanging onto their arms."

> prisoners who have the hope; This very day I am declaring that I will restore double to you.
> (Zechariah 9:11-12 ASV)
>
> Thus saith the Lord of hosts; In those days it shall come to pass, that ten men shall take hold out of all languages of the nations, even shall take hold of the skirt [garment] of him that is a Jew, saying, We will go with you: for we have heard that God is with you.
> (Zechariah 8:23)

Esther could sense a well of bitterness springing up in Bart's heart and silently she prayed. She knew that the nation Israel had suffered much through the centuries...and she knew that this Millennial Age was one in which the people of Israel would rightfully receive the promises God had long ago made to them through their forefather Abraham.

> And I will make of thee a great nation, and I will bless thee, and make thy name great; and thou shalt be a blessing:
> And I will bless them that bless thee, and curse him that curseth thee: and in thee shall all families of the earth be blessed.
> (Genesis 12:2-3)

Somehow, just somehow, she would have to wash away the well of anger in Bart's heart with a double portion of love.

Bart was seated in Phil Sutherland's office in New York. Phil had called George Omega in Jerusalem and said that he needed Bart. Something had come up and Bart was great on research. "It will get Bart's feet wet in this industry," Phil assured a doubting Omega. George had been reluctant to have Bart travel so quickly after his honeymoon.

Phil Sutherland seemed to have changed in the past few months. Bart got the impression that he was no longer the dedicated believer which he had at first appeared to be. Bart hesitatingly questioned him about this.

"Bart," Sutherland leaned back on his chair slowly, as though thinking of how best to express his feelings...

"Bart, I must admit there was once a time when I did not love the memory of my Aunt Carole, Harry's wife. But then, one day, I read her old diary and suddenly I realized that she was a precious jewel. Then when I asked Uncle Harry, he, with tears, told me of that day at the Valley of Jehoshaphat...that day when God condemned my aunt whom I never saw to an eternity in..." his voice trailed off in bitterness.

"And the Jews...sure I can appreciate their suffering...but I've suffered, too...the Arabs have also suffered. I've read about

"I've seen their miserable refugee camps after the 6-Day War."

their miserable refugee camps after the 6-Day War. And I've also seen the rich, haughty self-righteous Jew in Manhattan... with his maids, his butlers, his chauffeurs. I've seen one hypocrite step on the lives of my friends...who were believers...just so he could reach the top of the heap...over their dead bodies. Then he went around sanctimoniously 'preaching Christ.'"

"But, Mr. Sutherland, Phil," Bart interrupted, "doesn't forgiveness and turning the other cheek enter into this?"

"Turning the other cheek?" Sutherland let out a sarcastic laugh. "I've turned a hundred cheeks...but when I learned that my own aunt was sent to Hades...that was it! Look Bart, suppose you woke up one day and found that Esther had been sent to the Lake of Fire...not for a day...not for a year...forever. Understand that...forever! Slowly suffering FOREVER. AND THERE WAS NOTHING...no, NOTHING YOU COULD DO ABOUT IT!"

Bart Malone whitened.

"Bart, let me show you what's in store for those of the nation Israel. Pick up that Bible there. Turn to Isaiah, chapter 61. Now read aloud verses 5 and 6."

Bart began to read:

> And strangers will stand and pasture your flocks,
> And foreigners will be your farmers and your
>   vinedressers.
>
> But you will be called the priests of the Lord;
> You will be spoken of as ministers of our God.
> And will eat the wealth of nations,
> And in their riches you will boast."

"Hear that, Bart, one of these days World Television Network may be taken over by the nation Israel. And you, you'll be out tending cattle somewhere in the Plain of Esdraelon...not for your benefit...but for theirs!"

Phil Sutherland could see that the point was just about hitting home. Bart Malone would make a good partner in his future plans. But he had to make sure.

"Another verse, Bart. Read Isaiah 49:22-23!"

Bart continued reading:

> Thus says the Lord God.
> Behold I will lift up My hand to the nations,
> And set up My standard to the peoples;
> And they will bring your sons in *their* bosom,
> And your daughters will be carried on *their* shoulders.
>
> And kings will be your guardians,
> And their princesses your nurses.

"They will bow down to you with their faces to the earth, And lick the dust of your feet."

They will bow down to you with their faces to the earth,
And lick the dust of your feet;

There was more, but Bart could go no further. He knew now the life ahead would not be easy. And he and Phil Sutherland were going to change it!

For the Resurrected Believers, such as Tom Malone, Bill Sanders, Helen, Sue and Tommy Omega, the Millennium was not a time of testing. They had already been through their testing years prior to the inception of the Millennium...and they had seen themselves as sinners and turned in faith to Christ for forgiveness. Now they were righteous and completely fulfilled in Christ.

And although they were having a part in the millennium, they were on the earth, in a sense, as co-rulers with Christ, having duties to perform which they did eagerly. They loved the theocratic government and they cooperated with everything without resentment.

It was natural for them to approve of all that Regent David and the others did, because their eyes were looking (as it were) from the top of the Master Weaver's pattern...seeing the design in all its perfectness.

While underneath, George Omega, Faye Sanders, Terry Malone, Bart and Esther Malone, Sylvia Epstein and Harry and Phil Sutherland were seeing the apparent mismatch of tangled threads that to them spelled disorder, and in some created jealousy and dissent.

How often Tom Malone wished that for one brief moment he could show his loved ones the other side. Yet each time he approached Terry and quoted such familiar verses as:

...we know that all things work together for good
to them that love God,
to them who are the called
according to His purpose. [1]

There hath no temptation taken you
but such as is common to man;
but God is faithful,
who will not permit you to be tempted
above that ye are able,

---

[1] Romans 8:28

"Tom, darling, I'm sorry, I'm so sorry...oh Tom, I need you so much...forgive me...I'm sorry."

but will, with the temptation,
　　also make a way to escape,
　　that ye may be able to bear it. [1]

...these verses appeared to have no effect on Terry. Then Tom
would always add:

In everything give thanks;
　　for this is the will of God in Christ Jesus
　　concerning you. [2]

"It's easy for you to quote verses," Terry shouted...as though
Tom was hard of hearing.

"You can give thanks in everything...because everything's
going your way. You have no problems. You're resurrected.
You have it made. It's I that have the problems. I've got to face
the everyday life. I've got to wipe away Esther's tears...try and
straighten out Bart's misgivings about the Millennium. And I
have no one to turn to. You're no longer a husband to me. You
resurrected believers with that holy glow about you. And those
Jews running around with the Gentiles doing all the dirty work...
Do you call this justice? In some ways, everything is so perfect
here it's driving me crazy. Every place I turn I see holy trash
cans or holy dishes. Why even the smoke is holy anymore! And
everyone hanging on the coattails of Jews as they flock to the
Temple—as though each Jew was the President of the United
States or something. I can't go on like this. I can't go on. I've
counselled and counselled with Bart and Esther. Esther is so
sweet...so understanding...but Bart...it's like suddenly he has
been born of the devil!"

Suddenly the horror of her words hit her in the pit of the
stomach as though all the morning sicknesses of all her
pregnancy had come at one time. She felt weak and completely
drained. She burst into uncontrollable sobs repeating over and
over again...

"Tom, darling, I'm sorry, I'm so sorry...oh Tom, I need you
so much...forgive me...I'm sorry."

As they prayed Tom knew that it was all in God's perfect
hands now. And Tom could see the orderly pattern of His plan.

---

[1] 1 Corinthians 10:13.　　　　[2] 1 Thessalonians 5:18.

He could also see the underneath...and he knew some tangled threads would provide even greater sorrow before perfect peace ever came to those he loved so dearly.

* * *

Abdin Palace in Cairo was a scene of much activity. Phil Sutherland, George Omega and Bart Malone had flown there to televise what was to be an impending news event.

Hassan Ahmed, Governor of Egypt, briefed the trio on the problem. Old hatreds were arising among many of the youth born during the Millennium, Ahmed related. Some of the rebel Egyptians were exercising great influence now in the government...and they resented what they believed was preferential treatment of Jews in this Millennial Age.

Once a year a pilgrimage was to take place to Jerusalem. They objected to the fact that all edicts and all laws came out of Jerusalem. And to pay homage, by sending bowing delegations yearly to Jerusalem...this was too much.

The rebels sought to have a dual center of worship...one in Jerusalem, but one also in Cairo.

They ran through the streets of Cairo whipping up its residents in a frenzy shouting:

"Do you want to lick the dust off the feet of the Jew? If you don't, then join us in our protest march to Jerusalem. Stand up for your rights!"

> And many people shall go and say, Come ye, and let us go up to the mountain of the LORD, to the house of the God of Jacob; and He will teach us of His ways, and we will walk in His paths; for out of Zion shall go forth the law, and the word of the LORD from Jerusalem.
> (Isaiah 2:3)

Ahmed threw his hands up in the air: "What can I do? I am only the Governor. I cannot fight all these people. I'm afraid we're headed for trouble. All these years Egypt has been blessed with prosperity. Our lands have never been so fertile...our crops have never been so productive. The rains have watered our deserts. Now they blossom with every kind of fruit and vegetable. Whenever the season became dry...God, as though He was watching us every day, sent forth the refreshing rain. Now, I don't know what will happen...but what can I do?"

Phil Sutherland smelled trouble...and a good story...so he

and George and Bart flew back to Jerusalem to cover what was sure to be a conflict of important magnitude.

* * *

Never had Phil Sutherland seen so many people in the Temple area. The spacious central square was filled. Everyone sensed something important was about to occur.

The word had gotten out that Egypt was going to refuse to worship the Redeemer King. Part of its leadership had made a decision to formally protest...even though most of the people of Egypt did not concur with the action of this segment of their leaders.

Hassan Ahmed looked out of place. Yet he felt that he had to follow through. He had only to turn around to meet the angry stares of his rebel government. There was no backing out. At last he knew how Pilate felt in that judgment hall...knowing that what he was about to do was wrong...but yet, too weak to take any other stand.

Ahmed eloquently made his plea to Regent David.

Regent David began to speak:

> You are saying that Egypt, filled with all the
> blessings given by your Redeemer King...Egypt
> is refusing to bow down in worship?
>
> Do you realize the import of your decision? That
> such a decision is high treason against God
> and the penalty is swift?

Ahmed spoke quietly:

"Yes, my gracious Regent. My leaders have made this decision. This year, we will not enter the Temple to make our sacrifice of memorial. This is the decision of Egypt."

Suddenly all eyes focused on the Temple. It was a massive structure. Pillars on each side of the porch appeared to be 100 feet high. The doorway was some 43 feet wide. [1]

Facing us was the doorway to the east. The inner wall's eastern entrance was closed six days of the week...but open on the Sabbath.

---

[1] A complete description of the Millennial Age TEMPLE can be found by reading Ezekiel, chapters 40 through 48.

Suddenly a glorious light appeared from the east. Noise ceased as an overpowering presence was felt.

George Omega was telecasting some color descriptions when this unusual phenomena appeared. He began to shout...

"There is nothing wrong with your television set. What we are hearing is almost like the roar of rushing waters...the entire landscape in Jerusalem is lighting up as never before.

And without any given signal... suddenly everyone is burying their face in the dust of this Temple area. I have never witnessed anything like this before. Hassan Ahmed and his rebel leaders appear like helpless waifs in a violent storm. All color has been drained from their faces. They are the only ones standing...standing in amazement and in confusion. Listen...I think Regent David is about to speak..."

> **And behold the glory of God of Israel came from the way of the east: and His voice was like a noise of many waters: and the earth shined with His glory.**
> **(Ezekiel 43:2)**

> AND IT WILL BE
> THAT WHICHEVER OF THE FAMILIES OF THE
>
> EARTH DOES NOT GO UP TO JERUSALEM TO
> WORSHIP THE KING,
> THE LORD OF HOSTS,
>   THERE WILL BE NO RAIN ON THEM.
>
> AND IF THE FAMILY OF EGYPT DOES NOT GO
> UP OR ENTER,
>   THEN NO RAIN WILL FALL ON THEM;
>
> IT WILL BE THE PLAGUE WITH WHICH THE
> LORD SMITES THE NATIONS
> WHO DO NOT GO UP TO CELEBRATE THE
> FEAST OF TABERNACLES. [1]

Suddenly a burst of even more brilliant light shot out from the eastern entrance and Hassan Ahmed and his delegation vanished. It had been as though a laser beam had brought

---

[1] Zechariah 14:17-19.

sudden destruction on them. Where they stood was now an empty courtyard! [1]

* * *

It was a trying day and George, Phil and Bart hurried back to the apartment to wash off the dust of the day and to get ready for dinner.

Terry and Faye were busy in the kitchen. Both decided they would cook Bart and Esther's favorite dishes.

Both had spent much time in Beirut and Baalbek. They had roamed hand in hand through the mountains of Marj Uyun and through the Cedars of Lebanon. They called this their "Little Bible Land." For while it had been in the middle of much conflict in past history, it was now blessed with God's special outpouring on its fertile lands.

Bart and Esther loved the food of the Lebanese. And often, they longed for those succulent dishes.

Esther had taught her mother how to make *kibbeh.* Esther taught her and Terry both how to combine the lamb meat with *burghul* — crushed wheat.

"Where did you find this dish, Esther?" Terry asked.

"Bart and I were in Zahle in Lebanon. If you ever want to eat great *kibbeh*...the finest is made and served in the restaurants of Zahle!"

"Here, Mom, you pound the wheat and lamb for a while... then just knead it and season it."

After the initial work was done, Bart came in, lifted up some of the raw mixture with his fingers and plunged it into his mouth.

"Bart, you're eating that RAW!" Terry shrieked.

"It's ok Mom, we've often eaten it raw. It's called *kibbeh nieheh* when raw."

Faye ground the chick peas, added olive oil and a few other ingredients for another appetizer dish Esther called *hommus.*

The wrapped grape leaves, the fried eggplant, the shish kabob ...all made that night a memorable evening...a lull before the storm.

---

[1] Isaiah 11:3-4; Numbers 16:19-35.

Bart had become increasingly restless over the recent events. The people of Egypt were suffering because of a lack of rain. Phil Sutherland had purposely sent Bart to cover these events for World Television Network.

> No longer will there be in it an infant who lives but a few days, Or an old man who does not live out his days; For the youth will die at the age of one hundred And the one who does not reach the age of one hundred Shall be thought accursed.
>
> **(Isaiah 65:20 ASV)**

Bart never could erase that one picture of an Indian, who had migrated to Egypt, carrying his dead wife...emaciated. He had never looked hunger in the face before. He had never seen anyone die because they did not have enough to eat. Now, everywhere he turned...he witnessed the tragedy and the stench of famine...God's judgment.

And this was just one more event that boiled the cauldron of bitterness within him. He was afraid soon that this cauldron would boil over!

Bart reported back to Phil Sutherland at his Jerusalem office.

"Mr. Sutherland, Phil, from your own reading and study do you think that the tribulation period could have been as bad as this? Was the battle of Armageddon as tragic?"

"Bart, down the centuries many warriors of many nations passed back and forth upon the stage of Esdraelon. George Adam Smith in his classic *Historical Geography of the Holy Land,* published way back in 1894, wrote:

> The elephants and engines of Antiochus,
>   the litters of Cleopatra and her ladies,
> the Romans who come and plant their camps
>   and stamp their mighty names forever on the soil...
> Pompey, Mark Antony, Vespasian and Titus,
>   pass at the head of their legions,
> And the men of Gaililee sally forth upon them
>   from the same nooks in the hills of Naphtali
>   from which their forefathers broke with Barak
>   upon the chariots of Canaan...
> ...then the ensigns of Christendom came.
> Crusading castles rise...

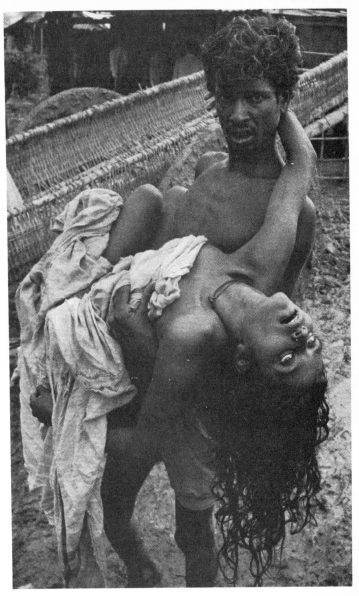

He had never looked hunger in the face before. Bart never could erase that one picture of an Indian, who had migrated to Egypt, carrying his dead wife.

Once more by Bethshan the Arabs break the line
of the Christian defence
and Saladin spreads his camp
where Israel saw those of the Midian and the
Philistine...

Esdraelon is closed to the arms of the West
till in 1799 Napoleon
with his monstrous ambition of an Empire
on the Euphrates,
breaks into it by Megiddo,
and in three months again,
from the same fatal stage,
falls back
upon the first great retreat of his career.

"It was through Megiddo Pass that General Allenby's Australian cavalry came thundering into the valley in 1918 to break the back of the Turkish line."

Sutherland continued, "Over and over again through thousands of years, blood has flowed in battle for the possession of this strategic point of Megiddo. But the bloodiest was the Battle of Armageddon, Bart. Over 200 million were killed by the hand of the Lord. The blood bath covered over 185 miles!" [1]

Phil Sutherland could see anger suddenly flow into Bart's face...like a tide coming in on a peaceful beach...soon to erupt into a violent storm.

"Phil, you will never catch me licking the dust from off the feet of a Jew, even if it is Regent David! I may be confused... but I won't be confused for long. I'm going to do some research and I'll come up with an answer. Why should we Gentiles have to go bowing into Israeli Jerusalem? There must be another way. There's just got to be another way!"

Phil Sutherland's lips curled in a half smile. There must be another way, he thought, and he was going to help Bart Malone find it.

It was to be a way that would end in a destiny neither Phil nor Bart would have thought possible!

----

[1]Revelation 14:20; 19:19-21.

Chapter 8

THE SECRET at SODOM

Over 900 years had passed since Bart and Esther were united in marriage. It seemed like yesterday.

Age knew no limits in this Millennial Kingdom and they had the physical appearance and stamina of persons 25 years of age in the pre-millennial earth. Disease had been abolished and the tragedy of old age did not exist.

No labor strikes, no struggle to make ends meet...the normal problems and tensions of the 20th Century were not prevalent during this 1000 years.

> And the inhabitant shall not say, I am sick: the people that dwell therein shall be forgiven their iniquity.
>
> **(Isaiah 33:24)**
>
> No longer will there be in it an infant who lives but a few days, Or an old man who does not live out his days; For the youth will die at the age of one hundred And the one who does not reach the age of one hundred Shall be thought accursed.
>
> **(Isaiah 65:20 ASV)**

Through the hundreds of years since their wedding Esther noted a growing restlessness in Bart. In spite of a perfect kingdom ruled by the Redeemer King and Regent David, there was continually an atmosphere of uneasiness that surrounded her husband.

She was worried about his years of association with Phil Sutherland.

Esther, Terry, Sylvia and Faye were having a coffee break before taking a leisurely walk through the Garden of Gethsemane. This familiar site was still in Jerusalem and the trio

Terry was happy the Garden of Gethsemane was empty. They could be alone.

often found this place a quiet respite when tensions mounted.

"Esther, has Bart said anything to you lately about his upcoming trip to Sodom?" Terry questioned.

"Just offhand he mentioned he was going there with Phil Sutherland and Dad. Why?"

Sylvia put her arm around Terry. "Come on, Esther and Terry, let's go to the Garden and pray. God knows all about our problems. We'll solve nothing rehashing Bart's sudden change in attitude. Only prayer can change things."

Terry was happy that the Garden of Gethsemane was empty for once. They could be alone.

Tears came to Faye Sanders' eyes.

"Mom, why are you crying?" Esther asked.

"Honey, this place brings back precious memories."

"You mean when Christ prayed here before His crucifixion?"

"Yes, but also when Dad and I were running for our lives...

almost 1000 years ago...running from Brother Bartholomew. We knelt to pray. We thought we were all alone and free at last. But in the shadows of the Garden was Prophet Arthur, the False Prophet of the Tribulation Period. It was the beginning of a trail of tears for us...but God gave us the victory."

"Mom, Satan is now bound in the bottomless pit. Where is it?"

"Honey, we do not know. Perhaps it is the Black Hole in the sky that troubled scientists in the 1970's...a vast void that appears to have no end."

Sylvia, a completed Jew, loved to question Faye Sanders.

"Faye, just exactly who is Satan?"

And I saw an angel come down from heaven, having the key of the bottomless pit and a great chain in his hand,

And he laid hold on the dragon, that old serpent, which is the Devil, and Satan, and bound him a thousand years,

And cast him into the bottomless pit, and shut him up, and set a seal upon him, that he should deceive the nations no more, till the thousand years should be fulfilled: and after that he must be loosed a little season.

(Revelation 20:1-3)

"Satan is a fallen spirit, and an imitator...not an originator. He imitates completely the pattern and program of God. This is how he has fooled so many people. So successful was he originally that he fooled one-third of the angels of heaven into following him!"

> And his tail [Satan's] swept away a third of the stars of heaven, and through them to the earth. And the dragon [Satan] stood before the woman who was about to give birth, so that when she gave birth he might devour her child.
>
> **(Revelation 12:4 ASV)**

"That was his original rebellion. Do you realize that Satan was not only one of the wisest of the created beings but also one of the most beautiful. Ezekiel 28:13 describes his beauty...

> You were in Eden, the garden of God;
> Every precious stone was your covering:
> The ruby, the topaz, and the diamond;
> The beryl, the onyx, and the jasper;
> The sapphire, garnet, chrysolite;
> And the gold, the workmanship of your settings and sockets
> Was in you.
> On the day that you were created
> They were prepared."

"You mean to tell me Satan had all that...and he still was not satisfied!" Sylvia exclaimed. "I remember when my Abel bought me my mink coat. Wow, I thought that was seventh heaven!"

"No Sylvia, Satan was not satisfied. You see, God gave Satan ...as He gives us...a capacity to choose. Satan could have chosen this complete perfectness, but he chose to depart from it. Just as you and I have had that choice...and as those in the Judgment of the nation Israel and the Judgment of the Gentiles have had that choice. Remember, even one-third of the angels at one time chose to follow Satan."

"Faye," Terry interjected, "I remember back in my old Sunday school days our teacher outlined Satan's sins. If I can recall ...Satan's biggest words were I WILL!"

"That's right, Terry. There were five 'I will' statements by Satan. They are found in the Old Testament book of Isaiah, chapter 14, verse 13:

"I WILL ASCEND TO HEAVEN"
> Satan wanted to abide there *as* God!

"I WILL RAISE MY THRONE ABOVE THE STARS OF GOD"
> He wanted to usurp God's authority.

"I WILL SIT ON THE MOUNT OF ASSEMBLY IN THE RECESSES OF THE NORTH"
> Here Satan was expressing his desire to control all the affairs of the universe!

"I WILL ASCEND ABOVE THE HEIGHTS OF THE CLOUDS"
> Satan's glory was a *reflected* glory. His brilliance came from God's Light. But Satan wanted a greater glory than God's.

"I WILL MAKE MYSELF LIKE THE MOST HIGH"

"Can you imagine the sinful folly of that last statement? Satan was the wisest of God's beings. He was the most powerful. He could go from one end of the universe to another. But the fact that he was not omniscient (all knowing); he was not omnipotent (all powerful); and he was not omnipresent (present everywhere at the same time)...these facts built up in him a rebellious pride."

"Mom, Satan wasn't called Satan at that time, was he?"

"No, honey, before his fall his name was Lucifer. That means 'the light bearer' or 'the brilliant one.' It was an appropriate name then. And I recall reading somewhere in Scriptures that one day...in fact, one day soon, he will return as an imitation light bearer and fool many."

"Was Brother Bartholomew one of his followers?" Sylvia asked anxiously.

"Yes, Sylvia, Brother Bartholomew was the most powerful and cruelest man of the pre-millennial age...a man indwelt of Satan. And his influence will soon be felt again."

Terry began to weep Faye wondered what she had said to suddenly reduce Terry to tears. Somehow Sylvia seemed to understand what it was all about. She put her arm around Terry's shoulder and motioned to Faye to pray.

It has been a dusty trip to Sodom...but reports of some unusual occurrences had sent Phil Sutherland, George Omega and Bart Malone there in a hurry.

Phil had sensed that the mood of the people was changing.

"George, I've just completed a trip around the world. And I'm telling you that people are just fed up...all of this authority that comes right out of Jerusalem has them stirred. They want localized authority and power. They've had it...this 'under the thumb' pressure is too much. And those drastic judgments by a God you can't see...without benefit of a fair trial. It's discrimination in its highest form. Israel is getting everything and we're their servants. The lid's about to blow off. I can sense it."

"Phil, are you sure?" George questioned. "I haven't heard any rumblings, any protests."

"Of course not, they'd be crazy to protest. You see what happens. Poof...instant death. I tell you...it's all building up inside them. It'll be an avalanche of protest once the time is right. Then I dare that man on the throne to try and instantly wipe out millions. That's when He will sit and listen."

George was amazed at Phil Sutherland's growing bitterness. Yet Phil had never really acted like a steadfast believer. And this combined with his remorse over his aunt Carole who had been committed to Hades...all added up.

George turned to Bart.

"Bart, what has your research turned up on Sodom and these recent activities?"

"Well, Sodom goes way back into history...about 2000 B.C. when the Bible declared that it was destroyed and became part of what was known prior to the Millennium, as the Dead Sea. There were 5 cities in this southern portion of the Dead Sea area...Sodom, Gomorrah, Admah, Zeboiim and Zoar.[1] These were the 'cities of the plain.''

"This area, prior to Sodom's demise, was very fertile," Bart continued.

"Four Mesopotamian kings under Chedorlaomer considered it worthwhile to make war on these five cities. They captured Lot. But Abraham rescued his brother's son. The wickedness of Sodom and Gomorrah caused God to destroy them." [2]

"What have your recent findings shown?" Phil inquired.

"Just this. People in the settlement near what was once Sodom...that's in the area of Neot ha-Kikar...have reported some strange sights...an unusual man."

"What was unusual about him?" George asked.

"Unusual in that he is surrounded by an aura of light. Some here have called him an angel of light...a second Messiah. We've had other reports of his appearance. Time and distance don't seem to trouble him. First I got a report of his appearance in Santiago...a day later in Tokyo...another day in Nairobi...the next day in Anchorage...and at another time in Chicago."

George and Phil took this in thoughtfully, then George asked, "What's so unusual about that...with the speed of our passenger planes...that's not impossible!"

Bart responded quickly. "True, but how do you explain this? His activities appear to be increasing. Just yesterday we received reports he was in 5 different heavily populated cities throughout the world...all 3000 to 5000 miles apart!"

"And what's amazing is this...people who feel they have ailments of one kind or another report instant healings. People who were afraid to gripe before about theocratic rulership are finding that he's giving them a sympathetic ear...promising

[1] Genesis 14:2; Deuteronomy 29:23; Genesis 13:12.
[2] Genesis 14:1-12; 19:24-26.

"...Sodom goes way back into history...about 2000 B.C. when the Bible declared that it was destroyed and became part of the Dead Sea."

them that at the end of this time period...things will *really* be perfect...and that everyone will have a say in government. And they won't have to work, either. That's what they like to hear."

"But his big promise is this...no more annual pilgrimages to Jerusalem...and no more special favoritism to the Jews. They'll be treated like everyone else."

"I'm for that," Phil chimed in.

"But that's not all. Here's the turning point! You know how the lack of rain has turned Egypt into a famine area? Well, guess what?"

"What?" Phil anxiously asked.

Bart's face could not conceal his excitement as he shouted, "IT'S POURING CATS AND DOGS in EGYPT! And this man did it. He was there and he made it rain!"

"What's his name?" George questioned.

"The people are starting to call him, **PRINCE OF LIGHT!**"

"He must be an imposter," George cautioned.

"You're wrong, George," Phil replied. "If he were an imposter, he would have been killed instantly by God. These activities have been going on for some time ...now this rain. It's a miracle. THIS MUST BE THE TRUE GOD...this Redeemer King we've been worshipping for the past 1000 years...he is the imposter. Let's clear the network and give full coverage to the PRINCE OF LIGHT. I want him followed every step of the way."

And when the thousand years are expired, Satan shall be loosed out of his prison,

And shall go out to deceive the nations which are in the four quarters of the earth, Gog and Magog, to gather them together to battle: the number of whom is as the sand of the sea.

(Revelation 20:7-8)

"I've already called New York, sir, and suggested that. I knew that's what you would want," Bart replied.

"But," cautioned Phil, "Let me ask that we wait here. I've been told THE PRINCE OF LIGHT will be making a special appearance here...right at Sodom."

"If that's so...have the girls join us. They'll want to see this miracle worker, too."

Bart called Faye, Esther, Terry and Sylvia...filled them in on the background, and told them to drive to Sodom as quickly as possible.

* * *

Abel Epstein was no longer a proud man. He was in Hades... the unseen world...awaiting the Great White Throne Judgment.

How often he had kidded Sylvia when Sylvia tried to tell him about her Christ.

"Sylvia," he would say, "so I'll go to Hell...at least I'll meet all my friends there. We'll be so busy drinking, we won't have any time for regrets."

Yet, never before had Abel felt so helpless and so hopeless. Money had been his servant before. He could have anything he wanted. When he was sick...he summoned the best doctors... when he was restless, he hired an entire plane to fly him to Acapulco. He loved the warmth of light. His apartment was bathed in walls of luminescent light...and he could turn to any imaginable hue at the flip of a switch. "A hue for every mood," he used to boast to Sylvia.

Now, he had no idea where he was. The terror of complete darkness was punishment enough. Dark...dark...midnight dark ...pitch dark...eerie dark...a darkness so black that it conjured countless images of fright in his mind.

Instinctively, he would reach for a switch...hoping that all of this was a dream from which he would soon awake...a cruel dream.

But there was no switch. He found himself grappling helplessly in the air, reaching frantically...for a switch nowhere to be found.

The reality struck him time and time again. There was no switch. There would never be a switch. There was no light. There would never be any light. Just total and complete darkness.

How often he tried to talk and communicate with others. He would open his mouth but nothing seemed to come out. Was their sound coming out? He mouthed the words carefully...enunciating clearly. Then in frenzy...he shouted until his throat became hoarse...and yet no sound...and no reply.

Was Hades so big that the human voice found no reflecting wall to bounce back the sound?

He could not even hear himself. It was like talking in a vacuum.

First NO LIGHT
then NO SOUND

What else could there be?

He REMEMBERED and for a while this consoled him. He remembered *The Wall Street Journal.* It was in June, 1972 when he had first read about the Black Holes in space. Time Tunnels...that's what they called them. There were mysterious signals coming from these deep recesses of space. These signals were picked up by Explorer 42. He recalled that the computers related that the signals came from an object in our galaxy that was many thousands of billions of miles from earth. And what amazed the researchers was that this unknown object seemed to have a diameter *smaller* than that of the earth. Yet the energy it was producing made it 1000 times more powerful than the sun. Bewildered scientists named it Cygnus X-1. Some even believed it to be a time tunnel. [1]

What could this be? Abel searched his mind without any solution. Was this heaven? Would it become the Lake of Fire? He

**And death and hell were cast into the lake of fire. This is the second death [the lake of fire].
(Revelation 20:14)**

knew enough Bible to know that the Lake of Fire would become his next and final destination.

Or was Cygnus X-1 where he was right now...Hades?

Then, suddenly, his thoughts came back to Sylvia. He had taken her for granted. Women were to be used...that was his motto. He had cruelly taunted her about the bevy of beauties he had on a string, while Sylvia quietly went on praying for him. She wasn't perfect, he knew that. She loved money and the things it could buy. But the last few months she had suddenly changed

And if thy hand offend thee, cut it off: it is better for thee to enter into life maimed, than having two hands to go into hell,

[1] The Wall Street Journal, June 16, 1972.

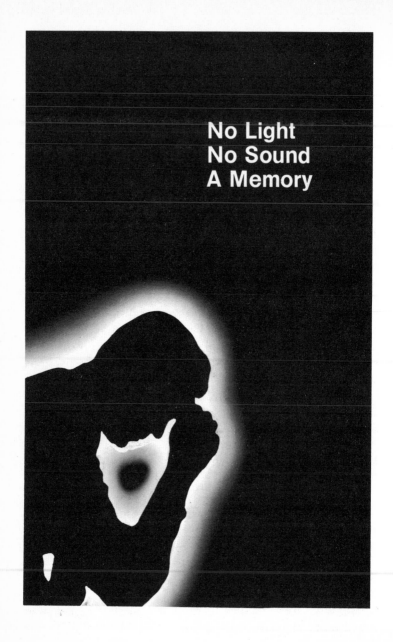

No Light
No Sound
A Memory

...and he loved her...oh, how he loved her. If only he could hold her in his arms...just once...and kiss her and tell her he loved her.

into the fire that never shall be quenched:
Where their worm dieth not, and the fire is not quenched.
(Mark 9:43-44)

The darkness seemed to carry a cloak of dampness that enveloped Abel Epstein. He cried but there were no sobs. The tears that normally would come...just never came. It was a hollow cry.

Suddenly he realized Hades had played a cruel trick on him. For not only now, but throughout eternity he would be plagued constantly with the torment of a MEMORY.

The picture the world had conjured up of the devil with a pitchfork constantly prodding everyone...this would be a relief, he thought to himself.

Facing him was a penalty far more unfathomable...

      NO LIGHT
      NO SOUND
      A MEMORY

* * *

By the time Faye, Esther, Terry and Sylvia reached the area of Sodom they found Phil Sutherland, George and Bart engaged in a very agitated conversation.

Something was wrong, the women could sense that.

Bart briefed the girls on what had transpired. The ladies were visibly shaken by what they heard.

Faye rushed to George...like a child suddenly seeking security from her father.

"Dad, can't you see what is happening? Satan has been loosed. We knew that this would occur at the end of the Millennium. And now that it's here...why aren't we recognizing it for what it is? Daddy, do something...don't let Phil and Bart get involved in this fantasy!"

It was a highly emotional scene. Faye was in tears. Sylvia, Esther and Terry look bewildered...and for the first time... frightened.

"It's not Satan," Bart blared out. "Can't you see we've been living under a rod-of-iron rule long enough. We've had it! Then when God finally comes around...we fail to recognize him as God. How foolish can we be?"

Esther clutched Bart tightly...not knowing what to believe... not willing to let him go. The world was falling apart around her ...and she felt helpless. Bart had changed during the hundreds of years of their marriage. Somehow now he was a more determined man. The judgments in Jerusalem troubled him. Lately he got to kicking the trash cans in the city sneeringly calling them, "Holy trash cans...you're no more holy than the trash I throw in them."

"Bart, honey, my mom and your mom went through so much. They lived in the Tribulation Period. They witnessed the terror and tragedy. Antichrist was far more severe in his judgments when you consider that he was a tyrant without righteousness. But now our Redeemer King has saved us from all of this...our every need has been supplied. There's been no more old age... no more sickness...no more poverty...."

She had said a wrong word...poverty. It struck a cord of responsiveness in Bart.

"Poverty? No more? Did you see the thousands in Egypt when they had no rain? Did you see the helpless babies crying until they could cry no more?...bellies bloated from famine? Well, I did. And who brought them rain...WHO? I'll tell you who...THE PRINCE OF LIGHT himself...HE BROUGHT THEM RAIN! That's what I call compassion. That's what I call love. That's what I call understanding...not a God who sends his edicts through David to administer. What makes David so self-righteous and above sin. Ask him about a cute, little Bath-sheba. Does he still look out the window from his high and mighty home? Every telephone pole in Jerusalem should be plastered with the Bible pages of Second Samuel, chapter 11."

Terry was hysterical. "Bart...that's enough...that's enough. STOP! STOP! I CAN'T STAND IT! I CAN'T TAKE ANYMORE! What's happening to us?"

Sylvia was also disturbed at Bart's sudden outburst. She thought that she would nip his beliefs in the bud by her question:

"Bart, what makes you so sure THE PRINCE OF LIGHT is God and not an imitation?"

Bart, now haughty and proud, realizing that he was winning his point poured out something he had not wanted to reveal... at least not yet.

"I haven't told Phil Sutherland or Mr. Omega this...because I didn't feel it was time. But now that you've asked...I'll tell you. I myself may not even understand the full import of it yet."

"The other day as I was walking alone in Jerusalem I was suddenly made aware of an unusual light coming in my direction. I looked up. There he was, THE PRINCE OF LIGHT! He was so beautiful. Never before...never, have I seen anyone so beautiful...as though every stitch of cloth on him was a shimmering, sparkling diamond...reflecting a light whose brilliance and beauty...well, it was just beyond description.

"What happened?"

"Well, he placed his hands on my head as though giving me a blessing and then said something I could not understand. He did not call me Bart or my full name, Bartimaeus. He said:

SON OF BARTHOLOMEW
IN THEE
WILL MY NEW KINGDOM RISE

"And in that moment, I knew I was annointed of God...but why, Bartholomew?"

Terry let out a piercing scream...rushed to Bart and fell, clutching his feet, sobbing uncontrollably.

Sylvia's face was ashen. "Bart, you fool. Terry went through a living death for you in the Tribulation Period. When your father, Tom, escaped with George and Faye...Brother Bartholomew promised Terry full pardon for Tom whenever they found him. But on ONE CONDITION. That condition was that Terry become his wife!"

"DO YOU UNDERSTAND THAT, Bart...HIS WIFE! Terry would do anything to save Tom. That's how much she loved him. In Brother Bartholomew's secret chambers she went through the wedding ceremony. Can you imagine the torture your mother was going through? CAN YOU IMAGINE?"

SON OF BARTHOLOMEW...
IN THEE WILL MY NEW KINGDOM RISE

"She never told anyone. I was Terry's closest friend in those days. And the irony of it was that...it was my Abel's ruby laser invention that Brother Bartholomew used to snuff out Tom's life instantly."

"That's why Terry told me alone, and only me, her secret."

Terry, half rising, her face bathed in tears, held up her hand helplessly, "NO, SYLVIA, NO, SYLVIA, please, please...." And then she lapsed into unconsciousness in a tangled heap at Bart's feet.

"It has to be told, Terry. I'm sorry. It's just gone too far. It has to be told."

"What has to be told?" Bart asked angrily because Sylvia was destroying all he hoped to build up by his recent revelation.

"This, Bart," Sylvia replied.

"YOUR NAME IS NOT BART. AND IT IS NOT BARTI-MAEUS EITHER. YOUR NAME IS *BARTHOLOMEW!* That's why Terry called you Bart...for short and let everyone believe it was short for Bartimaeus."

"I don't understand," Esther quivered.

"Let me put it in plain language. BART...is NOT Tom's son. *BART'S FATHER WAS NONE OTHER THAN BROTHER BARTHOLOMEW!*"

There was no more hiding the truth now. BART, who had been born in those first days of the millennium, *after* the great judgments of Israel and of the Gentiles, was the son of the man who had been the ANTICHRIST!

The secret had been revealed...at Sodom!

Chapter 9

POINT OF NO RETURN

George Omega had never seen Phil Sutherland so happy in the almost 1000 years they had worked together.

Phil had cleared the networks of World Television for a special announcement.

In a rather unusual procedure Phil advised the regular news commentator that he himself would make the announcement.

The studio had an air of excitement. The rumor had it that Phil had a special guest who would appear with him.

All but required personnel were kept out of Studio 1. Even George and Bart had to watch the proceedings on a monitor in another room.

Phil began his telecast:

> Ladies and Gentlemen:
> We stand at a momentous time in history.
> Perhaps no greater event can surpass what
> will soon occur!
>
> And to prepare you for the last opportunity
> for humanity, it gives me great pleasure
> to introduce...for the first time anywhere...
> on television...our Redeemer
> THE PRINCE OF LIGHT!

Looking at the screen in unbelief George could see that some form entered Studio 1, but it was hard to distinguish the characteristics. The light emanating from his body surrounded him in a halo which cast an eerie glow.

He began speaking...

VENGEANCE IS MINE
 I WILL REPAY
YOU HAVE OFTEN READ IN YOUR SCRIPTURES

> *FOR YET IN A VERY LITTLE WHILE,*
> *HE WHO IS COMING WILL COME.*

> *REMEMBER THE FORMER DAYS,*
> *WHEN AFTER BEING ENLIGHTENED*
> *YOU ENDURED A GREAT CONFLICT OF*
> *SUFFERINGS*

HOW MUCH SEVERER PUNISHMENT DO YOU THINK HE WILL DESERVE WHO HAS TRAMPLED UNDER FOOT THE SON OF GOD...

IT IS TIME FOR NATIONS TO ESTABLISH THEIR OWN GOVERNMENT AND TO OVERTHROW HE WHO WOULD CALL HIMSELF The Messiah!

THIS MESSIAH HAS GIVEN ISRAEL A SUPERIOR POSITION OF AUTHORITY AND THEOCRATIC RULE FILLED WITH UNJUST ACTION.

HOW LONG WILL GENTILES BE TENDERS OF CATTLE AND SLAVES TO THIS SO-CALLED SUPERIOR RACE?

BEHOLD I HAVE COME TO DO THY WILL!

AND THE VOICE OF MY PEOPLE HAS TOLD ME THE TIME FOR VENGEANCE HAS COME!

WITH ONE HEART AND ONE VOICE LET US MARCH ON JERUSALEM.

AND WHEN THE BATTLE IS WON, WITH JUSTICE FOR ALL, LET US BEGIN A NEW HEAVEN AND A NEW EARTH IN PEACE AND EQUALITY.

As quickly as it began...the TV special was over and Phil Sutherland began giving the background commentary and a call for action.

Bart turned to George: "George, this is the real thing. Did you hear all those Scripture Verses THE PRINCE OF LIGHT quoted from the tenth chapter of Hebrews?"

George looked dismayed. "Bart, just because someone quotes Scripture, that doesn't make him a Believer...let alone the Messiah. Even Satan can quote Bible verses!"

But there was no talking to Bart. George had spent hours trying to explain what was happening but Bart seemed gripped by an unknown power.

> And Moses and Aaron went in unto Pharaoh, and they did so as the Lord had commanded: and Aaron cast down his rod before Pharaoh, and before servants, and it became a serpent.
>
> Then Pharaoh also called the wise men and the sorcerers: now the magicians of Egypt, they also did in like manner with their enchantments [secret arts].
>
> (Exodus 7:10-11)

When Bart arrived home in Jerusalem, he found Esther in tears. Never had he seen her so emotional. As soon as he came in the door Esther got down on her knees, grabbed Bart around the legs and pleaded with him.

"Bart, please turn back before it's too late. Can't you see what you're doing to our marriage? You're turning your back on God in order to accept an imposter...that's all this PRINCE OF LIGHT is...an imposter. Bart, sit down with me and let's read the Scriptures."

Bart had a mind of his own...but one last time, he would go through the motions just to please Esther.

Esther opened her Bible.

"Look, Bart, the PRINCE OF LIGHT is none other than Satan himself. From the moment of his downfall, Satan has set himself in opposition to God. To unfallen man in the garden of Eden, he appeared in the guise of a serpent.[1] He was behind the universal corruption and consequent judgment of Noah's day.[2] He tempted David to number Israel.[3] Then there was the murder of the Hebrew babies in the time of Moses.[4] Some of these actions on the part of Satan were an attempt to blot out the line through which the Redeemer was to come."

Bart looked on unimpressed.

Esther continued: "In the time of wicked Queen Athaliah, an attempt was made to destroy the whole of the royal house. It was only through the intervention of his aunt, Jehoshabeath, and the fidelity of Jehoida, the priest, that the sole survivor, the young King Josiah, was preserved...thus continuing the royal messianic line.[5] And look what happened when the Messiah was born. Satan sought to destroy the children of Bethlehem through Herod.[6]

> **And his tail swept away a third of the stars of heaven and threw them to the earth. And the dragon stood before the woman who was about to give birth, so that when she gave birth he might devour her child.** (Revelation 12:4)

"Satan tempted our Lord when He was about to enter His public ministry. In fact, Satan personally took over in this temptation from the pinnacle of the Temple.[7] Then Satan entered into Judas Iscariot, hoping at last to achieve his purpose.[8]

"In fact, in what appeared to be Satan's greatest victory, at Calvary, the Christ of God turned defeat into victory. He undid the works of the devil,[9] annulled his power,[10] and defeated him who had the power of death."

"If all this were true," responded Bart, "then Satan would have no power now. He would be a helpless and defeated weakling. Therefore our PRINCE OF LIGHT is not Satan. He is our Redeemer and God. And this one you call Redeemer King is losing his power. He must be Satan!" Bart spoke firmly in his belief.

"No, Bart, you're wrong. You are twisting the Scriptures. Despite Satan's fall after the Battle of Armageddon he is still the ruler of the air. He's been bound

> ...ye walked according to the course of this world, according to the prince of the power of the air [Satan], the spirit that now worketh in the children of disobedience. (Ephesians 2:2)

---

[1] Genesis 3:4-7. [2] Genesis 6. [3] 1 Chronicles 21:1.
[4] Exodus 1:16. [5] 2 Chronicles 22:10-12. [6] Matthew 2:16.
[7] Matthew 4:1-10. [8] Luke 22:3. [9] 1 John 3:8.
[10] Hebrews 2:14.

in the bottomless pit these 1000 years by God. Now God has released him for a season."

"How can you believe such nonsense, Esther? Now tell me, why would God bind Satan for 1000 years and then let him go? Why doesn't He let Brother Bartholomew go, and Prophet Arthur, the two you have labelled as the Antichrist and his False Prophet? You've told me they're in the Lake of Fire forever. Yet they were only tools of this person you call Satan. If God were going to let anyone go...He'd let these two go. He certainly wouldn't let the chief criminal on the loose again. Don't you understand, Brother Bartholomew is my father. And I'll do anything to make sure he gets to Heaven. And the PRINCE OF LIGHT promised me this would be his first action after we overtake the government of Jerusalem."

"Don't you understand," Esther pleaded, "the millennium is not the final and perfect state of this world's history. It's the last of a long series of Divine periods during which man in the flesh is being given opportunity to turn from his sin to God. It is also in some ways the severest test of all, because it is a condition of privilege higher than man ever enjoyed before! What I'm trying to say is that this is the final test of fallen humanity under the most ideal circumstances!"

"Esther, I've had enough. There's just too much work to do. You're so religious you just can't see the light when it finally hits you. Your mother and Sylvia have been feeding you a bunch of fairy tales. You..."

The ringing of the phone cut the conversation short.

"It's Phil Sutherland. He wants me to get out to the Plain of Esdraelon on the double. The armies of the world are assembling there for their invasion of Jerusalem. Now look, Esther, get out of this place. Fly to New York with your mother, Sylvia, and my mom. Your dad is already there. I'll meet you there when it's all over. Don't just stand there...move!"

"Bart, what are you doing? Are you out of your mind? You're a pawn in this Prince of Darkness' wicked game. Bart, don't you see I love you. I love you, Bart! I love you! Don't go, Bart. Please don't go. If you go...I may never, never see you again. Oh

"Armies of the world are assembling there for their invasion of Jerusalem."

...Bart...puleeese...puleeese, darling...Bart. BART! STOP! STOP!...STOP!"

* * *

This was to be the PRINCE OF LIGHT'S triumphant hour. On World Television Network he had issued the call for volunteers to join his Victory Army. Even he was surprised at the response. When asked the count, Phil Sutherland replied, "It's just impossible...why the number appears as great as the sand of the seashore! This is a real success!"

And when the thousand years are expired, Satan shall be loosed out of his prison,

And shall go out to deceive the nations which are in the four quarters of the earth, Gog and Magog, to gather them together to battle: the number of whom is as the sand of the sea.

(Revelation 20:7-8)

Even after living in 1000 years of prosperity, wealth, without sickness and very little death...an abundance of everything... the PRINCE OF LIGHT was still able to accomplish the raising of an army **as numerous as the sand of the sea.**

Bart was inwardly happy when he heard this. Soon victory would be here and his father would be reunited with him. What a reunion! The invasion of Jerusalem would be accomplished in a matter of moments.

* * *

Esther, Faye, Terry and Sylvia were down on their knees praying in Esther's apartment. Their hearts were heavy with sorrow. Esther was heartbroken...her prayer broken by uncontrollable sobs.

Suddenly the whole sky appeared emblazoned in a red fury. It looked like fire was shooting out of the heavens beamed at selective targets on earth. Explosions rocked the foundation of their home.

Then as quickly as it came...it disappeared. And there was silence. Utter and complete silence. It seemed as though the world suddenly stood still.

Faye and Terry knew it was all over. God's judgment had come down on the onrushing army at

And they went up on the breadth of the earth, and compassed the camp of the saints

the outskirts of Jerusalem. She knew that all of the rebels had been wiped out by fire from Heaven.

about, and the beloved city [Jerusalem]: and fire came down from God out of heaven, and devoured them.

(Revelation 20:9)

There was no need to tell Esther. Sylvia could see the agony of this truth etched out on her face. Millions of people suddenly consumed by fire. It seemed unbelievable. But she knew it was true.

Esther, put on a light sweater and decided to go out for a walk. She left unnoticed as Faye, Terry and Sylvia were on their knees in prayer.

Esther walked through the Inner City, pausing briefly at Golgotha.

She walked through the Inner City, pausing briefly at Golgotha, then down Jaffa Road, past Ben Yehuda...then outside of the city limits. The warmth of the sun gave her an inner peace. She was walking...walking but not knowing where.

The events of the past whirled through her mind and she began talking, not realizing she was talking outloud. So stunned was she from recent experiences that she failed to realize each question she posed was being answered.

"What will happen to my Bart? Where is he?"

The span of God's patience is ended. He has waited long for sinners to repent and accept His grace.

Bart will appear at the Great White Throne judgment.

AND I SAW A GREAT WHITE THRONE, AND HIM THAT SAT UPON IT.[1]

IT IS A FEARFUL THING TO FALL INTO THE HANDS OF THE LIVING GOD.[2]

"But he seemed good. He didn't mean to do what he did. He was deceived."

THERE IS NONE RIGHTEOUS, NO, NOT ONE.[3]

A MAN IS NOT JUSTIFIED BY THE WORKS OF THE LAW...[4]

ALL MAN'S RIGHTEOUSNESSES ARE AS A POLLUTED GARMENT.[5]

"But can't he change his mind now? Now that he is...now that he is standing before God...can't he change his mind? Now he must realize that the PRINCE OF LIGHT was Satan. I'm sure he does. Now he knows who is God!"

AT THE LAST JUDGMENT IT IS TOO LATE TO START BELIEVING.

THE BOOK OF LIFE WILL BE OPENED.

"And what will happen?"

IF ANYONE'S NAME WAS NOT FOUND WRITTEN IN THE BOOK OF LIFE, HE WAS THROWN INTO THE LAKE OF FIRE.[6]

"No, not my Bart. Not Bart. Please, not Bart!"

---

[1] Revelation 20:11. [2] Hebrews 10:31. [3] Romans 3:10.
[4] Galatians 2:16. [5] Isaiah 64:6. [6] Revelation 20:15.

Esther fell to the ground...weeping. And as she looked up...a sign post came into view. She hadn't seen it before. On it... EMMAUS!

"Lake of Fire! What will happen to Bart there?"

> *IT IS A FIRE WHICH CANNOT BE QUENCHED.* [1]
> *THERE SHALL BE WEEPING AND GNASHING OF TEETH.* [2]
> *THERE IS NO PEACE TO THE WICKED.* [3]
> *THE SMOKE OF THEIR TORMENT GOES UP FOR-EVER AND EVER; AND THEY HAVE NO REST DAY AND NIGHT.* [4]

"I can never stand it...eternal separation from Bart. My whole life in Heaven will be one of eternal regret."

> AND HE SHALL WIPE AWAY EVERY TEAR FROM
>   THEIR EYES;
> AND THERE SHALL NO LONGER BE ANY DEATH;
> THERE SHALL NO LONGER BE ANY MOURNING,
>   OR CRYING,
>   OR PAIN:
> THE FIRST THINGS HAVE PASSED AWAY. [5]

Esther must have walked about seven miles from Jerusalem. It suddenly dawned on her that she had been talking...and someone else was providing answers. When she realized this she stopped and there beside a lonely olive tree, instinctively she fell to the ground...weeping...and as she looked up...a sign post came into view. She hadn't seen it before.

On it...EMMAUS!

She ran all the way back to Jerusalem...burst into the room where Faye, Terry and Sylvia were praying.

Startled, the trio looked up, imagining that the heat of the day and the judgment of fire, had disoriented Esther.

---

[1] Mark 9:43, 45, 48. [2] Matthew 25:46. [3] Isaiah 57:21.
[4] Revelation 14:11. [5] Revelation 21:4.

Esther shouted, "This earth will pass away...a New Heaven and a New Earth will appear...a New Jerusalem with no need of sun or moon...nor even a Temple!"

Faye wondered outloud: "If only Bill could be here. Somehow, I believe that he and Tom Malone and Helen, Sue and Tommy, are aware of all these events. Won't it be a grand reunion to be really back together again...no more separation...no more we with natural bodies and they with resurrected bodies. Soon all of us will have resurrected bodies!"

> And I saw a new heaven and a new earth: for the first heaven and the first earth were passed away; and there was no more sea...
>
> And I saw no temple therein: for the Lord God Almighty and the Lamb are the temple of it.
>
> And the city had no need of the sun, neither of the moon, to shine in it: for the glory of God did lighten it, and the Lamb is the light thereof.
>
> **(Revelation 21:1,22-23)**

There was a tinge of regret in Terry's voice: "Yes, but our family will not be complete...with Bart not...." her voice trailed off.

Sylvia, still picturing Abel with his money belt having been thrown down at the feet of the Redeemer at Kadesh-Barnea understood Terry's regret.

* * *

George, rushing in from a flight from New York, interrupted their conversation.

"OK, everyone, let's hop in the car. You need a change in scenery. Let's take a ride towards Bethel."

When George started the trek...he suddenly realized that the change in scenery would not be a pleasant one.

The impact of the judgment of of fire was seen everywhere. Like the plagues of Egypt the judgment had been selective. Only certain homes were destroyed...with those, who had followed The Prince of Light, dead. Some whom George thought were fol-

> And Moses stretched forth his rod toward heaven: and the Lord sent thunder and hail, and the fire ran along upon the ground; and the Lord rained hail upon the land of Egypt...
>
> Only in the land of Goshen, where the children of Israel were, was there no hail.
>
> **(Exodus 9:23,26)**

lowers of the Redeemer King to the end..some of his closest friends...were objects of judgment from the fire that emerged from Heaven. They, apparently, had been among those as numerous as the sands of the sea who had cast their lot with the false Messiah.

George wanted to turn the car back...but he realized that it was too late. Already the damage had been done. Perhaps, he thought, their actually seeing this disaster of death, might prove a blessing.

Soon it appeared they could go no farther. Groups of men were carting off bodies and traffic jams were building up.

George decided to turn around and go back home. Just then Esther screamed, "There's Bart. There's Phil!"

She jumped out of the car and ran to a pile of bodies. She saw two men lifting bodies tying their hands and feet with a cord.[1] She grabbed the arms of one of the men shouting, "STOP, STOP!! What are you doing? That's my husband. That's Bart! Oh, my poor, poor Bart...what have they done to you?"

She heard a familiar voice and looked up. The two men were Bill Sanders and Tom Malone.

Faye ran over to be with Esther, her daughter. Never had she seen her so distraught. The scene was too much for everyone. The judgment was too terrible for the eye to behold. Phil Sutherland, Bartholomew Malone...lying there dead!

Faye tenderly placed her arm about Esther, and spoke, "Esther, honey, God will make us to understand later concerning that which still troubles us about His judgments. It is impossible for us as living believers fully to understand all of God's dealings. He tells us...

> As the heavens are higher than the earth, so are My ways higher than your ways, and My thoughts than your thoughts."[2]

"I cannot understand God as Creator. His works are infinite. My eyes can scarcely fathom them, much less explain them. Nor do I understand God as Saviour. His love is inconceivable. His mercy toward us surpasses all our imagination. How then, can

---

[1] Matthew 22:13.   [2] Isaiah 55:9.

Esther saw two men lifting bodies. She grabbed the arms of one of the men shouting, "STOP, STOP!! That's my husband!"

I understand Him as Sovereign Judge! But the moment is soon coming, honey, when we shall know even as also we are known.[1] Then, what today seems bewildering in the plan of God will be made perfectly clear to us."

Esther looked up at her mother, somehow understanding. "Mom, 1000 years. I thought it would be a long time...but it was just a moment...a split second of eternity...how can anyone trade a few short years of sin to forfeit an eternity with our Saviour? What a reunion that will be...a reunion that will never end!"

Then Esther took one last look at Bart's lifeless body. No one will ever know the regret that swept through every fiber of her being.

As if to say goodbye, she held Bart's hand. From it dropped a crumpled note.

> Dear Esther...my whole heart's
> desire is to be forever with you.
> Love,
> Bart

"Poor, darling Bart," Esther cried..."Oh, Bart, how I wish a million times it could be true. But it can't be true...never, darling, never."

And Esther was right.

For Phil Sutherland...

For Abel Epstein...

For the millions who had made Satan their god throughout the ages...

And for Bartholomew Malone.

They had reached the point of NO RETURN!

---

[1] 1 Corinthians 13:12.

EPILOGUE

The long day of night has ended.

And the eternal day without night has begun.

Satan, after the Millennium, has been cast into the Lake of Fire to join Antichrist and the False Prophet forever (Revelation 20:10).

The unsaved dead, after the Millennium, are then raised from the dead in what commonly is referred to as the "second resurrection" (the first resurrection being when the believers were raised to life eternal with Christ) — (Revelation 20:5-14).

Then — the saddest verse of all:

> *And whosoever was not found written in the book of life was cast into the lake of fire.*
>
> (Revelation 20:15)

All the saints of all the ages are now resurrected believers living in their glorified bodies eternally with Christ.

For living believers, George Omega, Faye Sanders, Terry Malone, Harry Sutherland, Sylvia Epstein and Esther Sanders there is a glorious reunion with Helen Omega, Sue and Tommy Omega, Tom Malone and Bill Sanders (resurrected believers).

For George, Faye, Terry, Sylvia, Harry and Esther now take on a new glorified body as they enter the New Jerusalem.

Together they enjoy forever throughout all of eternity a life with

1. NO NIGHT
   There will be night there. Christ will be the light that illumines that City (Revelation 21:25).

2. NO TEARS...NO DEATH

There will be no more tears in Heaven. There will be no more pain in Heaven. There will be no more sorrow, no crying in Heaven. There will be no more death in Heaven!

   ...God shall wipe away all tears from their eyes; and there shall be no more death, neither sorrow, nor crying, neither shall there by any more pain: FOR THE FORMER THINGS ARE PASSED AWAY. (Revelation 21:4)

3. NO MORE SEPARATION

All the saints of all the ages will be there. No more will friends have to part again. No more will the Malones and the Omegas and Sanders have tearful farewells. No more disagreements. No more misunderstandings with our loved ones! Together they will rejoice in everlasting joy and companionship.

The 1000 years of Millennium were just a pause on the vast panorama of eternity.

And if you could look ahead, into the window of heaven, you would see George and Helen Omega, Bill and Faye Sanders and a host of their friends rejoicing in the eternal joys that will be theirs forever.

And for Esther...whose husband, Bart, will spend an eternity in the Lake of Fire...there is equal joy in the New Heavens and the New Earth...for "...the former things shall not be remembered or come to mind" (Isaiah 65:17).

> The false and empty shadows
>   The life of sin, are past —
> God gives me mine inheritance,
>   The land of life at last.
> 'Tis finished — all is finished —
>   Their fight with death and sin!
> Fling open wide the golden gates,
>   And let the victors in.

Chapter 10

THE CHOICE

You have just read *1000*.

Remember, in the introduction to this book, I said that undoubtedly many who read it will consider it an interesting science-fiction story.

IT IS NOT!

This book deals with LIFE and DEATH.

Your life...or your death!

While the book *1000* was written in novel format the facts of the 1000 year MILLENNIUM PERIOD and the judgments ...are true!

You will recall throughout the book are numerous Scripture references directing you to the Bible for specific events and judgments.

Now, you must face up to a CHOICE.

And the main question is this:

WHAT WILL YOU DO WITH JESUS?

Will you state that He never existed?

Will you simply say that He was a good man who did good things...like many other good men?

Will you say His message is not relevant to our enlightened age?

Your decision should not be based on what your friends or

relatives say or do not say...or on your own private concept of heaven or hell. These really, in the final analysis, *do not matter!*

What is important...and what will govern your tomorrow in ETERNITY...is WHAT DOES THE BIBLE SAY? In light of God's standards, set forth in the Bible, your final destiny will be determined.

You can, as many do, simply choose to ignore Christ and the Scriptures...go on living your life, doing the best you know how to meet your problems, work to provide an income for your family, set aside a nest egg for retirement...

But THEN WHAT?

What happens when it comes time for you to depart from this earth?

Then WHAT WILL YOU DO WITH JESUS?

It takes NO DECISION on your part to go to Hell!

It **does** take a DECISION on your part, however, to go to Heaven!

> He that believeth on Him is not condemned:
> but he that believeth not is condemned already,
> because he hath not believed in the name of the
> only begotten Son of God. (John 3:18)

Whether you are Jew or Gentile, here are five basic observations in the Bible of which you should be aware:

1. ALL SINNED
> For all have sinned, and come short of the glory of God. (Romans 3:23)

2. ALL LOVED
> For God so loved the world, that He gave His only begotten Son, that whosoever believeth in Him should not perish, but have everlasting life (John 3:16)

3. ALL RAISED
> Marvel not at this: for the hour is coming, in which all that are in the graves shall hear his voice.
>
> And shall come forth; they that have done good, unto the resurrection of life; and they that have done evil, unto the resurrection of damnation. (John 5:28,29)

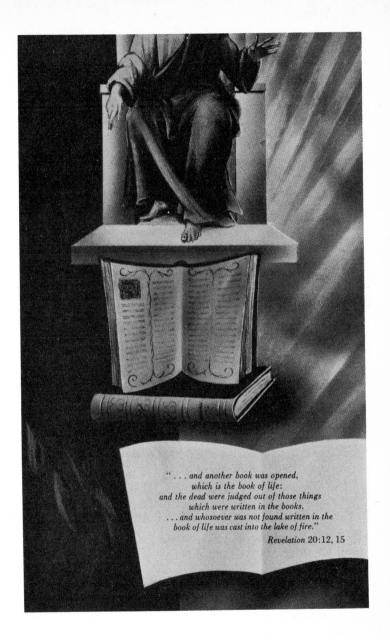

" . . . and another book was opened,
which is the book of life:
and the dead were judged out of those things
which were written in the books.
. . . and whosoever was not found written in the
book of life was cast into the lake of fire."

Revelation 20:12, 15

4. ALL JUDGED

> ...we shall all stand before the judgment seat of Christ. (Romans 14:10)

> And I saw the dead, small and great, stand before God; and the books were opened...(Revelation 20:12)

5. ALL SHALL BOW

> ...at the name of Jesus every knee should bow... (Philippians 2:10)

Right now, in simple faith, you can have the wonderful assurance of eternal life.

Ask yourself, honestly, the question....

WHAT WILL I DO WITH JESUS?

Will you accept Jesus Christ as your personal Saviour and Lord or will you reject Him?

This you must decide yourself. No one else can decide that for you. The basis of your decision should be made on God's Word—the Bible.

Jesus tells us the following:

> "...him that cometh to me I will in no wise cast out...

> Verily, verily I say unto you, He that believeth on me hath everlasting life"—(John 6:37,47).

He also is a righteous God and a God of indignation to those who reject Him....

> "...he that believeth not is condemned already, because he hath not believed in the name of the only begotten Son of God"—(John 3:18).

> "And whosoever was not found written in the book of life was cast into the lake of fire"—(Revelation 20:15).

YOUR MOST IMPORTANT
DECISION IN LIFE

Because sin entered the world and because God hates sin, God sent His Son Jesus Christ to die on the cross to pay the price for your sins and mine.

If you place your trust in Him, God will freely forgive you of your sins.

> "For by grace are ye saved through faith; and that not of yourselves: it is the gift of God:
>
> Not of works, lest any man should boast"—(Ephesians 2:8,9).
>
> "...He that heareth my word, and believeth on Him that sent me, *hath* everlasting life, and shall not come into condemnation: but is passed from death unto life." (John 5:24)

What about you? Have you accepted Christ as your personal Saviour?

Do you realize that right now you can know the reality of this new life in Christ Jesus. Right now you can dispel the doubt that is in your mind concerning your future. Right now you can ask Christ to come into your heart. And right now you can be assured of eternal life in heaven.

All of your riches here on earth—all of your financial security —all of your material wealth, your houses, your land will crumble into nothingness in a few years.

And as God has told us:

> "As it is appointed unto men once to die, but after this the judgement:
>
> So Christ was once offered to bear the sins of many: and unto them that look for Him shall He appear the second time without sin unto salvation." (Hebrews 9:27,28)

Are you willing to sacrifice an eternity with Christ in Heaven for a few years of questionable material gain that will lead to death and destruction? If you do not accept Christ as your personal Saviour, you have only yourself to blame for the consequences.

Or would you right now, as you are reading these very words of this book, like to know without a shadow of a doubt that you are on the road to Heaven—that death is not the end of life but actually the climactic beginning of the most wonderful existence that will ever be—a life with the Lord Jesus Christ and with your friends, your relatives, and your loved ones who have accepted Christ as their Saviour.

It's not a difficult thing to do. So many religions and so many people have tried to make the simple Gospel message of Christ complex. You cannot work your way into heaven—*heaven is the gift of God to those who have their sins forgiven by trusting in Jesus Christ as the one who bore their sin.*

No matter how great your works—no matter how kind you are—no matter how philanthropic you are—it means nothing in the sight of God, because in the sight of God, your riches are as filthy rags.

"...all our righteousnesses are as filthy rags...."
(Isaiah 64:6)

Christ expects you to come as you are, a sinner, recognizing your need of a Saviour, the Lord Jesus Christ.

Understanding this, why not bow your head right now and give this simple prayer of faith to the Lord.

Say it in your own words. It does not have to be a beautiful oratorical prayer—simply a prayer of humble contrition.

My Personal Decision for CHRIST

"Lord Jesus, I know that I'm a sinner and that I cannot save myself by good works. I believe that you died for me and that you shed your blood for my sins. I believe that you rose again from the dead. And now I am receiving you as my personal Saviour, my Lord, my only hope of salvation. I know that I'm a sinner and deserve to go to Hell. I know that I cannot save myself. Lord, be merciful to me, a sinner, and save me according to the promise of Your Word. I want Christ to come into my heart now to be my Saviour, Lord and Master."

Signed..................................

Date..................................

If you have signed the above, having just taken Christ as your personal Saviour and Lord...I would like to rejoice with you in your new found faith.

Write to me...Salem Kirban, Kent Road, Huntingdon Valley, Penna. 19006...and I'll send you a little booklet to help you start living your new life in Christ.

JUDGMENT DAYS

RAPTURE
BELIEVERS meet CHRIST in the air

REWARD JUDGMENTS FOR BELIEVERS

"and I will dwell in the house of the Lord for ever." (Psalm 23:6)

INCORRUPTIBLE CROWN (Victor's Crown)
". . . every man that striveth for the mastery is temperate in all things . . . they do it to obtain a corruptible crown; we an INCORRUPTIBLE." (I Corinthians 9:25)

CROWN OF REJOICING (Soul Winner's Crown)
". . . what is our hope . . . or crown of rejoicing? Are not even ye in the presence of our Lord Jesus Christ at His coming? For ye are our glory and joy." (I Thessalonians 2:19, 20)

CROWN OF RIGHTEOUSNESS
"Henceforth there is laid up for me a crown of righteousness, which the Lord, the righteous judge, shall give me at that day: and not to me only, but unto all them also that love His appearing." (II Timothy 4:8)

CROWN OF GLORY (Crown for Service)
"Feed the flock of God which is among you . . . (be) examples to the flock. . . And when the chief Shepherd shall appear, ye shall receive a crown of glory that fadeth not away." (I Peter 5:2-4)

CROWN OF LIFE (Martyr's Crown)
". . . the devil shall cast some of you into prison, that ye may be tried . . . be thou faithful unto death, and I will give thee a crown of life." (Revelation 2:10)

"Every man's work shall be made manifest . . . because it shall be revealed by fire . . . if any man's work abide . . . he shall receive a reward . . . if any man's work shall be burned, he shall suffer loss: but he himself shall be saved; yet so as by fire." (I Corinthians 3:13-15)

GOLD	PRECIOUS STONES
SILVER	

1000 YEAR MILLENNIUM

JUDGMENT OF UNBELIEVERS

BOOK OF LIFE

THE BOOKS OPENED

"And whosoever was not found written in the book of life was cast into the Lake of Fire." (Rev. 20:15)

". . . the tares are the children of the wicked one: The enemy that sowed them is the devil: the harvest is the end of the world; and the reapers are the angels. As therefore the tares are gathered and burned in the fire; so shall it be in the end of this world." (Matthew 13:38-40)

LAKE OF FIRE

THE RESURRECTIONS

Heaven

Resurrection and Ascension of Christ into Heaven (Matthew 27:52-53 tells of others who were resurrected after Christ—these were the wave-sheaf of the harvest to come. Leviticus 23:10-11.)

Acts 1:1-11
Matthew 27:50-53

Paradise

Believers who have died before the Rapture. Present in a celestial, spiritual body. *

"And Jesus said unto him, Verily I say unto thee, To-day shalt thou be with me in paradise." Luke 23:43

"We are confident, I say, and willing rather to be absent from the body, and to be present with the Lord." 2 Corinthians 5:8

Believers meet with Christ in the air 1 Thessalonians 4:16

"...the dead in Christ shall rise First:..."

"Then we which are alive and remain shall be caught up together with them in the clouds to meet the Lord in the air:..." 1 Thessalonians 4:16-17

Judgment Seat of Christ

"For we must all appear before the judgment seat of Christ......" 2 Corinthians 5:10

Believers now in New Bodies Philippians 3:20-21

Resurrection of Tribulation Saints Daniel 12:1-2

Marriage of the Lamb Revelation 19:7-9

Christ Returns to Earth with His Saints 1 Thessalonians 3:13; Zechariah 14:4

"And I saw the dead, small and great, stand before God; and the books were opened; and another book was opened, which is the book of life: and the dead were judged out of those things which were written in the books, according to their works.

And the sea gave up the dead which were in it; and death and hell delivered up the dead which were in them: and they were judged every man according to their works." Revelation 20:12-13

Great White Throne

"And whosoever was not found written in the Book of Life was cast into the Lake of Fire." Revelation 20:15

Resurrection of the Dead Unbelievers Revelation 20:11-13; Jude 6

Unbelievers cast into Lake of Fire eternally

| About A.D. 30 | This Present Age | A.D.? | Rapture | Seven Year Tribulation Period | Mount of Olives Armageddon | 1000 Year Millennial Age | With Satan Antichrist and False Prophet |

* Physical body remains in grave awaiting Rapture

Copyright © 1973, Salem Kirban